According To Helen

Ω

a
Mike Gutowski
novella

A mind numb is a head empty.

The Open

Truth is a friend who everyone remembers differently. There's time. Somewhere, there's more time. It may not be found where we expect, but it's out there. The problem for humans remained the same. They're humans. Their usual has always been a crazy place, and the unknown even more so.

In there, in the mind kettle, strange potions bubbled and boiled, released steam and balmy air, then cooled, spread aromas, quelled emotions, parried in facts and fictions until a rest screamed frothy, usually cycled to the sun's will, and finally folded of a darkness claimed in retreat. Such is life on the Brim planetoid.

Popular songs of the time spouted repetitive doom mantras in major population areas. Retreat wasn't a place for answers, surrounded by pricks of regrets and rationalizations. While the body rested the mind continued relentless attacks. Such a living and breathing circumstance served as foundation for communities small and large of inhabited human, humanoid, creature, or otherwise. Syntax and grammar were damned in the process as language of voice and body mingled into an undertaking spiced of survival needs. The lazy atmospheric haze hovered as conqueror in that glaze where much horror lived masked.

Horror loved darkness. Lived it. Breathed it. Created a shield. Provided cover. A place to hide, and plan, and rest. And scheme. The sunshine didn't dare go there anymore. It's hard enough to find people who care about themselves much less anyone else. For what was coming, that circumstance they noted, served the future. It knew we were fools playing at being human. Easy to trip up, deserving a fall.

Find the place where horror slept and kill it. Such a waste it creates in the mind box. Distracts. Disinfects. Rejects the rational. Some say no cure for it. A fool's game search, it is, to seek it and extinguish it. It existed as much intertwined in the human biology and psyche as edible and audible needs. Find the seed and murder it. Eliminate offspring. Such a curse, to hunt and kill. Ill will and nasty themes resided infectious.

She told me many stories about life when I was a child, my great aunt Helen did, while I remained seated directly facing her at a summer kitchen table located in the back of her rowhouse. My dad had dropped me off at her home before he went out with his uncle to tend to various neighborhood matters mysterious. I could hear their voices as the sounds attempted to penetrate the red brick exterior, but in no manner could I interpret or decipher the meanings of their words. My mind simply wouldn't answer the call for any quarter to comprehension attempts.

All outside sounds disappeared, faded into the ether, while her voice calm, yet puzzled in tone, recounted to me various odd efforts presented to her and her family when she was a child. I thought the stories strange at first, but my mind stewed on them many months later, then years later, until it became her time to pass.

While she lay in the hospital upon her death bed, my cousin invited me into great aunt Helen's room, for a last visit, but seemingly more as a means of hope that I could translate what she tried to say during the moments of her last breaths. One last piece of wisdom or insight I searched for, tried to glean from her strained forehead and facial expressions. No understanding availed itself, and that circumstance made me feel bad.

Something hidden inside her mind popped forward as a premonition, as it did many times before during our times together. Premonitions cursed her mind. It dug whole into her mysterious past. I could tell, as a child, she presented a watered-down version of the horrors she recounted. Her voice and tone served as a salve in my attempts to understand meaning, then, and more so now.

"Deceits," she said to me, perhaps as a means to voice one last clue of a future sentience not yet discovered. I tried to read her lips; her voice toned as far away while the cover of the oxygen mask betrayed her vocalization efforts. Memory mind schemes toiled long, were uttered humble of voice. I asked, "Aunt Helen, what are you looking for?"

"Not looking. Searching." She responded in this manner many times, trailing nuances gently from her thin lips.

"For whom? For what?" I wondered then, and still now.

Her creased lips struck forward, shaped out like a small dark hole, as whispers escaped.

"You." She tried to reach out to me, but her nearest hand remained restricted by a wormy hospital fluid drip hose.

Current events dragged me back to those childhood days. Memories of her home and outer environs beamed more relevant to this present time. Something I missed, it seemed, along the connection route between then and now. In the narrow pathway between the collection of rowhouses, neighbors and casual strangers traveled on foot, to grocery shop, converse about past day event matters, or worse, night matters, exchanged knowledge tidbits related to housekeeping, cooking tricks, and toils financial or otherwise cloaked in mystery matters. Words passed among my ears quickly during those times permitted to spend with her. My mind housed voices of ghosts evidenced by passings of many years. Wisdom traded, bartered back and forth, hidden in the voices. Preparations banter ruled the verbiage cycles on the streets, in the alleys, uttered in desperation tones. Ghosts of the past traversed the same paths.

Not enough time for nonsensical banter, yet banter sometimes ruled the day, perhaps to allow the minds to unload the complexities of their lives into the garbage heap of regrets dropped into the alley where a heavy rain and sailing wind would wash them away. Simple talk, in hushed voices. Exchanges of facts, rumors, food recipes. Sometimes I was allotted an overnight stay at Aunt Helen's when my dad and uncle's neighborhood adventures fell over into the next morning. In the spare room obliging the service of one window sucking in night light beams, my analysis of night sounds as means to eliminate mysterious natures and machinations unfolded. Whirlwinds of thoughts no hand could grasp, and a mind scream ensued, "What is truth!" Sounds and corner of my eye spotted motions convinced me of a spirits and ghosts presence amidst the room's parameters.

Did the previous day progress as expected, or was it small in stature and prominence. Splattered, splayed wide by the horrible unexpected? Resolutions to such wonders deemed necessary a promotion safety, survival. At least, coveted for a one more day existence moment.

When everything seemed together snug, the fine times tipped all towards moments of frenzy and chaos yet to commence. Expectations of such calamities lay secreted between the populace perception lines, the bricks, the sidewalks, the dark corners jutted from a building's edge. Perhaps she perceived my development into adulthood, from her deathbed, still lacking in purpose. On the cusp of my first visit to Aunt Helen's house, my dad told me she knows much about life. Listen carefully. You will eventually understand. I listened much to her words which sometimes pursed upon her lips long, followed by near inaudible mutters, but the mutters achieved a rhythm over time into my ears, and the sounds eventually roamed around in my head until some sentience to their meaning became revealed. Sometimes like new knowledge bites and other times as wisdoms elegant amidst Matisse waves soft of stroke captured from a palette's origin, then transferred in form to a lonely canvass.

Perhaps wisdom she shared in watered-down condition, sensing my child's brain needed understanding assistance. I wondered because as I grew up and acclimated more so to the complications of humanhood, a realization of the left out found details stunned me at times expected and otherwise, in dreams, in nightmares. In the horrid happenstance of what she had told often I realized a truth in the deeds of another's actions, whether they be someone I knew, or some public figure popularized or polarized by the shady band of media acolytes looming forward from the tech presentations of my later years.

But here it was, now, that moment perhaps she had warned me about, and due to my lack of understanding, failed in preparation for. Hauntings come in many flavors. It's the way of the human. Other creatures learn through instinct, repetition, and develop an efficiency essential to survival. Hauntings don't exist in their being quotient, to serve as distraction of reality and sentiment. Sentiment kills. A slow and miserable death it is in the creature world. So, it has been struck out of mind through evolution methods. A self-brainwashing seemed necessary. Hauntings distracted learned instincts into the shadows.

I asked my cousin what was great aunt Helen saying. He said the best he could produce, after he had listened to her verbal sounds for an hour, was "one day I will find you when regrets are many." My cousin didn't know if she was speaking to him or about someone else whose face came randomly into her mind during her death breath moments. Perhaps the subject of her attempted vocalizations was her deceased spouse, or one of her sisters, or the great uncle who suffered war-time prison camp life.

The Davosian Days

In the Davosian planetary era, breathing became a right regulated by a necessity measurement. Heralded as a blessing, it had evolved into a curse upon the population of remaining humans, humanoids, and other creature inhabitants. The natural evolution of government deemed many living organisms of necessity vacant, required no further societal usage space.

At first, the daily edicts only applied to organisms below human or humanoid classification. Hybrids were not exempted. The hybrid population grew stoked by environmental disorders; survival needs. Gradually, a few, then more than a few, then many humans and humanoids became named as unnecessary. Such a permission granted tracking rights for those willing to cooperate with the Davosian regime. Captures brought enhanced living conditions mainly interpreted as food sources. Hybrids started a revolt born of survival instincts. Some humans and humanoids rallied to their cause.

According to government edicts, hybrids disturbed the natural order. The government determined the meaning of natural order, on a daily basis frequency. Generally, every living thing that was not government approved or licensed didn't have a right to breathe. The planetoid atmosphere had been polluted gruesomely by the last world war. Rationing had become the order of the day, down to the breathing cycle. That cycle was controlled by food sources distributed by the government. Day only existed as a gray fog haze. Night existed as a somewhat darkened day.

The government placed blame for these living circumstances upon unruly and unauthorized living entities. Making examples of resistance attributed to biological creatures, the government proceeded to lock tight the vault housing their power structure. Hybrids regularly defeated such life restriction notices, and made mockery of the government's power and life grabs.

All of the living world the government claimed for itself, rationalized by a need for imposed order efficiency upon all living things due to collapsed environmental harmony. The government tricked the populace into committing crimes through the use of daily edicts which measured worthiness and utility. Edicts were posted on stable objects like poles, mature trees, brick or frame walls of which few remained completely intact; and through announcements loudly blared from strategically placed loudspeakers at known population centers.

Many of the larger known populations at first ignored as inconsequential the admonitions and interventions of governmental institutions. Towns of lesser means stopped hearing announcements as the government tended to not maintain the audible systems properly. Some believed such a life-altering condition was intentional. Eventually, the survival scales tipped in favor of the government. Gradual surrenders of larger populated centers dropped in line first after suffering the ad nauseum governmental pressures, at great cost to those in the centers not willing to cooperate.

Each loudspeaker activation praised, "War is over. Life begins again." For many in the population, the war never ended. The time of it seemed eternal and ongoing. So too, "Progress is Purpose" posters and signs were plastered and papered over on many visible surfaces in varied sizes large and small as a reminder of the new freedom. Protesters, now disappeared, painted over the words "War" and "Life" and wrote "Life is Over. War begins again." Also reversed the second government mantra so it read "Purpose is Progress."

In a reality not officially government recognized, freedom existed only for those in control, and such control stunted existence potential for those not government owned or sanctioned either in lifestyle, deed, and word. Freedom inhibitors the non-government beings were not. Those not government authorized to exist, deemed no longer useful, unnecessary, suffered for it. Disappeared.

To miss the edict presentation, usually in early morning hours, could result in an immediate death sentence or disappearance determined by the government overlords' needs of that particular day. Their needs lived insatiable.

Truth had died at the first spawn of the new gray light. Since that time, unless truth had merely run away to hide from the realities of time, the days and nights here have remained a gray of varied shades and forms. All creatures human, humanoid, hybrid or otherwise, searched for it, truth, by trial-and-error methods. Gruesome outcomes prevailed regularly, but through practice, some predictable regularities were discovered.

The unusual had always been a crazy place, and the unknown even more so. Obviously, near everyone of purpose or curious cause wanted to try a visit there. Right and wrong laid as a spread of peanut butter and jelly, or apple butter, thin upon an otherwise pedestrian twosome of bread personalities. Pizza served supreme as dinner warm and dessert newlyweds sweet. Truth had been relegated to the status of a hungry beggar.

Loneliness involved holding onto a memory everyone else had let dissolve into the time mists. There existed consequences for knowing and consequences for not knowing. Choose the travel road to not much and none. Nations were no longer built on a foundation of Reason. The Age of Ignorance ruled. Murder and mayhem was so prevalent here you'd think it was taught as part of the usual public school education curriculum.

Many betrayals does it take for humans, humanoids, hybrids and other creatures to no longer trust each other or themselves. We can only ask the dead. The dead know all. Their voices long gone, long silent, ceased even as whispers. Persecution will make that business nasty. Those old whisper voices were government outlawed amongst the remaining populace to hear or accept further.

The recent dead, worshipped as revolutionary heroes, still echoed voice sounds in the new Brim world populace. Conjurers of the long dead existed, but of necessity, in the darkest of shadows available in this gray Brim world. The new government sponsored short histories. The new histories eliminated wisdom from long ago, excised lessons learned in the old Brim world, dissolved perspective into silent screams. No need for old wisdom. It would only conflict with new wisdom. The new wisdom treated dissent as indecency.

The leader of the new wisdom had a name. It became the name for death itself over time, as actions spoke louder than the printed words on government sanctioned signage. He, if it existed as a he, was neither living nor dead, but both, a soluble part of the in-between, not vampire or spirit, but each and all, connected to all, a piece of all, part god and part demon, but not all of either.

The rumors of his horrors perpetrated, now only reported in whispers, described his mere essence as ether itself, an invader of bodies, minds, and souls, unifier of each and divider of all, ignitor of sour words and dour thoughts, aggravator in chief, agitator individually. He is Daed Suoregnad, the one no one wants to meet. He decided the day, time and place of every single meeting of thought, deed, and future.

Dormant in time processes since before time existed in the human, humanoid, hybrid, creature and plant realms, yet alive as mythical evil construct; a convenient and programmed story necessary before any invasion but sentient in purpose to find an energy source upon which to feed. A big bang he detected, then migrated towards such energy releases, until the stars of a new universe attracted his attention. Brilliant in mind tempered raw by the darkest of hearts. No foul or fair deed survived his moral relativities, a poison locomotive fueled by hopeless energy.

The soothsayer, Helen, knew all of these events, trials, tribulations of the existence meanings unbalanced since the day of her birth. They flowed in and out of her mind, only to be revived close in time to relevant purpose. At first, through small releases of trapped knowledge imbedded in her subconscious genetically, but eventually triggered by human events encountered during the younger years of calculated fate moments.

When puberty hit, an explosion of the subconscious knowledge nuggets occurred, almost driving her insane by the intensity of the experience. Sisters Thelma and Wanda had preceded her, each imbued of essential abilities intelligent and physical as accompaniment to Helen's traits. They learned and taught each other as a coven of the secret knowledge, each tortured of premonitions of no apparent cause or meaning.

Practice and calculation of success; notes taken of facts and reality situations leading to conclusions about the world around them; and later after contact with other humans, humanoids, and creatures, predictive skills developed could accurately lead to foreshadowed events. Complements to the rare and unusual bounty bestowed upon them by heritage at birth.

Our perception of human nature has been poisoned, continuously, since the beginning of the hominid species Brim stone existence. Look at today's cultural and social paradigms. A similar course reveals itself. Discerning what is truth consists of ingredients claimed necessary to create a tasty stew, but the stew is spooned out for control of the population, costs a hefty price in surrender of the individual spirit. It remains a mystical endeavor cheap in cost for those in power, destructive to all others below such status. The fabric of life travels daily undermined in every moment and means of social contact.

The greed of the head hovered as unquenchable. The overlords heeded the call to feed the beast's needs. At first the weak of mind surrendered their kin and friends, then themselves of destroyed free will. The well-off in finances tried to buy themselves a continued pleasant existence, but eventually even their forced generosity failed, as the government assurances previously made gradually collapsed into the ashes of the beast's cooking pot fires. What remained existed now. A new Brim world, worse than the previous concoction, but still survivable for the creative of mind and sturdy spirit. Learn the rules. Develop a means around them. Breathe one more day. Every breath is precious.

According to Helen, a particular circumstance was threaded into all human, humanoid, creature time periods: "Don't hear it, absorb truth into being. Never know the tune of it. Exist lost in miasma's cruel spirit. Truth bends, shapes, bonds as relativity theory. Fantastical, fungible." Her skin color gray, texture tight, eyebrows bright in sheen, yet sadness couldn't help but project a crooked beam around the iris pulps. The power and extent of the knowledge she absorbed literally blinded her biologically into old age. Perhaps pulling down the shade was required to keep her mind healthy.

A god or gods made all things possible, including marijuana, to help the earth inhabitants survive blatant and horrible mistakes during the creation process. A ghoul, demon, or humanoid who is able to haunt to death those who wronged it, comes to mind. Like a ghost avenger. The shade threads were created by Suoregnad machinations. Great Aunt Helen could see through the shade while looking at it in the pulled down state. The other side spirit world shadows bore names, purposes, and uses for the living.

Renovations – Antillean Dances

Some humans freakout like it's their job and they get paid bonus for it. The Big Tech age sabotaged the patience angels of our minds. The enemy of my enemy is my friend pops out to me as literary jargon. In the living of real life, more likely, the friend of my friend is my enemy. Always become suspicious of a giver's gallantry, and too, the tenacity of a taker.

I woke up one day and looked out the window and realized an eerie silence had overtaken the below as far as I could see. I concentrated on a listen yet still was unable to catch any sounds into the inner ear canal. A deep and too warm temple's pounding alerted me to a fear rising up from my bowels. Not the usual hunger pangs. Just silence too long in tone. "What is this," I wondered. No bird noises, no squirrel ramblings to stir the roof shingles, no vehicles blurting mechanical bursts? Only a light wind at times, and tree branches swished the pleasant musical notes of leaf instruments. I requested my mind to make some sense of it. An unusually quiet moment for the neighborhood as if the objects and small creatures only existed, and not the two-legged occupants like myself.

There's a time frame for everything. The everything seemed out of smack, and wacky even. I tested my hearing, tapped on the inside window sill, and noises responded. I sniffed at the air after raising the window a bit, and the air seemed the same as usual. A hint of flowers bloomed, a touch of light upon all things, except a graveness tone to it all. I looked at my electronic clock on the table beside my bed until I could deduce whether it still functioned. Maybe a power outage. No such evidence. The clock wasn't flashing blue light off and on at the digital numbers. Curious.

The smallest moments of these events refused to open a path for greater understanding of the situation. The larger moments of the outdoors hid any reason for changes in the environment's usual daily progression. I combined these observations into my cranium bowl, stirred a few times, and hoped for some type of smoothness to develop, but none occurred. Just chunks unending and resisting a complete mix of the event ingredients, like a mashed potatoes blending effort. I previously had cracked and busted my potato masher while using it as a hammer after my conventional hammer head came loose from the handle long ago. Of course, that incident, not worthy of report, left me hammerless in any conventional fashion. Not enough pennies had been pinched to rectify the situation. I remain hammerless and potato masherless.

In a serious and continued effort to adjudge a situational understanding, I repeated a recon of the properties outside the window. Many cars were no longer parked on the street. Usually a few remained in the daytime, as most neighbors still worked jobs. Mine I no longer needed, so I sold it. Okay, that's not true. It broke down and I didn't have the money to fix it, so I had it junked. I remembered watching the tow truck driver hook up the chains to the rear wheels and crank the old bird onto the back of the truck's steel plating. A somber moment. A goodbye weary.

Anyway, I could use the walking exercise for grocery trips. Some essentials included beer, smokes, coffee, tuna fish, bread, mayo, salad dressing, relish, baloney as a treat when available, sandwich cookies, soup, soup, and more soup, oatmeal times two, apple or cranberry juice depending on availability, crackers, cracker dips, milk or a milk substitute, and the usual faux paper products like toilet tissue, napkins, and snot catchers. And more somber moments checking prices. Sometimes the journey lasts so long, the destination becomes an afterthought. The map is inconveniently worn or torn. Tumult beckons.

The Brim Load Cometh

The main character in my mind can see objects, insects, humanoid outlines as if spirits or ghosts, buzzy things floating and flashing in and around her almost constantly. Unless completely calm, at rest, in solitude, these distractions are memories or foreshadowing's which she, Aunt Helen, could spend all of her time attempting to interpret, but she must go on with her life, tend to necessities bubbling real, and side step imagination distractions. Her culture called the experience the Brim's edge, as the precipice of some event requiring interpretation for her to move forward on something of which she was uncertain. Perhaps a moment of her life or someone else's life. Or a circumstance critical in time to avoid success or disaster which could lease out worse circumstances either for her, local citizens, or the world as a whole.

She was vaguely schooled by a family familiar to such a kin's affliction in these circumstances of her individual existence, and further schooled in how to interpret them, but she never mastered the meanings or signs enough to satisfy her curiosity for a better understanding. And now it could kill her to fail a test of understanding or interpretation correctly. Clarification remained the unstruck piano key, the misplaced guitar string. Improperly tuned musical instruments toned wrong the present actions into future sounds displaced.

Are there truly elders or experts of this culture I could find to help me control the visions inherited by genealogical happenstance, or better understand them? Aunt Helen earned her call upon a stage she was too shy to step upon. So, she allowed me to transcribe her efforts. It remained, even into her old age, difficult for me to attain a fuller understanding of her voiced premonitions. At first, out of laziness if not carelessness, I omitted all of the words and sounds from my note-taking tasks. She scolded for such incompetence.

I deserved the scolding. Bettered myself during the tasks to determine whether these visions or scenes where in her head only, or was she sometimes drawing out of my mind what she could see and merely regurgitating the results, or both at the same time, or did the experience reside external to my mind, in actual reality, affecting the reality and environment around me.

Traveling a road of many signs, trying to determine significance of each. Where to find an interpreter for the signs? What religions? What god? What spirit travelers? A mere wandered, I seemed to my own mind. At best, and in the present time, I came upon the realization that every human, humanoid, creature society reached a precipice of extinction, teetered along the edge precarious, sometimes for eons of time if lucky, as long as hope and practices of regular and inspired ingenuity still remained as resources. Such is the circumstance in this Brim world. A place where existence teetered on the edge forged by too many mistakes.

Like my aunt, ghosted memory haunted my days and nights, mainly related to human, humanoid, creature encounters on the job or otherwise social in nature. I didn't know what had become of the memories in the new Brim, whether they disappeared, or joined the Davosian recruiting effort. Only three status levels of all beings currently existed.

Government workers, the disappeared, the about to be disappeared existence levels were the only ones viable on a planetoid destined for extinction soon, according to the government experts and based on what science says. Fear reigned as sovereign amongst all groups as kin to the Davosian overlords. The meaning of kin is a stretch, but all had been claimed as kin by the remaining financially powerful bold and brainy self-designated.

The controlling thread in all of these clans remained the threat of instantaneous recalibration of the social mix, either upward or downward or at the in between invisible. The numbers of invisible were never publicized. We knew who we were and sometimes where, but the whole point of such a cultural development was to follow the rule of safety, the place of judgments not severe or life-threatening.

These are the types of humans, humanoids, creatures I encountered while traveling along the Brim. I traveled for exercise and searches of food and water sources, and further to avoid entrapments into a most dangerous circumstance by devious persons, or groups. The environment acted like a prison. No need for societal imprisonment from my way of thinking. Premonition jiggered the mind, so alone time ruled as necessity. Premonition moments acted like hypnotic states of mind causing temporary paralysis of the body. The reaction was the bodies way to protect against detection of prowlers or those harboring ill-inclined intentions. The encounters to date list ensues.

Six A M- an energetic female, ready for anyone or anything that comes her way. Squelches problems like a person who continuously cuts-off the words, down to the syllable, of other speakers once a thought explodes amidst brain synapses. Her ocular activity could send the viewer into a tipsy state. She appeared human of high spirit, but bordered on a potential humanoid, meaning off world genes of unknown relation mixed into her family history.

Noon- a male, likely a humanoid, always half-way between here and there in thought and deed. Also, gene confusing issues. Humans had the weakest gene history, then humanoids were stronger in instinct intelligence and resilience, then hybrid creatures most powerful in physical strength and stamina but more forgiving in social circles, at least for a time. The current governmental systems strictly separated the groups based on gene pool, and only exploited each portion for punitive measures, for control purposes absolute.

Mass-a male who treated every day like a solemn holy moment never-ending. Also, a rather tall and wide physical presence. He was suspected of being a hybrid, but difficult to tell. Hybrids didn't speak of their origins much. The overlords had scrubbed their histories.

Midnight- a syrupy, romantic, never do well. Seemed to rather make a mistake during deeds and actions, than not act at all. Lots of scars this one bore of deed and need, as if suffering were an expected if not readily anticipated trait of existence. No looking back unless she lost an object or thought. She was a marvel to behold and experience. The humanoids got along with her well. Thoughts seemed to poke her in the neck, as she reached there often when her thinking voice was about to be uttered. A typical Midnight conversation, her starting the parry and my responses.

"Do you believe in love?"

"Sure, at six in the morning or whenever the Sun comes up over the horizon."

"No. Really. Do you believe in love?"

"No. Not at all."

"Why?"

"Too much 'why' about to fall."

"Too many falls. I get it." She gave me a side glance grimace, half-hearted one at that. Not a hybrid, I thought. They didn't concern themselves much in word parry. I furthered the parry.

"Much like a disease insidious."

"What?" She pursed her lips to drip out the word love, but thought better of the effort. She noticed my slight discomfort, in the right cheek of my jaw line. Awaited, she did, my word play to continue. Didn't take long for my rumination to evolve into a syllabic iteration, as per the usual course.

"A rather dour assessment, I'd say."

"Sure. I knew you'd say."

"Ah, a seer," I responded in a mocking tone.

My hope was to squelch her will to continue, at least along the verbalized path. She filed away this communication method, for later use.

She wanted to say, "No. Empty soul," or at least my mind imagined so after reading her facial expression unaccompanied by any auditory accompaniment, but declined further discourse. She didn't like how this tiny and insignificant banter scratched at prior emotional wounds; tried to bleed out some of her deeper thoughts, hidden in the place of her mind long ago sealed off. I calculated her responses and facial expressions as still human. Battered by life, but still strong of will and purpose.

Just memories now, some of these few I've met in the new Brim. Like Wind Souldiers, they are ghosts in the wind who helped to protect. Not all Wind Souldiers were soldiers in war. They served humanoids as protection spirits, although their ability to do so involved some physical machinations, primarily of object movement, including humanoids themselves as object, like moving them away from a moment in instances of danger. Their afterlife is believed to exist in a nearby solar system as a civilization living on the edge of that galaxy. Stories of the Wind Souldiers feats still seep into the new Brim.

In their ancient times, they rose up to defend their brethren and sisterhood on a nearby planet. Interestingly, their history mirrors our old Brim myths which have not yet disappeared. Some believe ourselves to be the foreshadows dwellers, the alternate planetoid system of Shadow Souldiers, a direct connection clan to the Wind Souldiers. My great aunt Helen tried to explain it to me as best she could. Not believing prevented me from having a complete understanding of her foresight abilities. I could deduce, not of sufficient certainty, the place I now reside is the old Brim undergoing at present a conversion.

Some information my brain ejects and then reinserts into my physical being follows regarding the background history of each civilization. Sometimes I have wondered if Helen was a genetic descendant of Shadow Souldiers.

One of the civilizations in Shadow Souldier lore is similar to Earth's origin story of Adam and Eve, except Adam and Eve were born on Mars, not Earth. Eventually, the evidence for such a connection wasn't made public. That Mars civilization died out but not before the inhabitants had traveled to Earth biologically, along with computer data to preserve the history. The data came encased in a special plastic type cylinder which when properly activated would reveal the history of Martian Adam and Eve, and once that connection is confirmed in evidence, a Holy War starts on Earth between the believers of Earth origin Adam and Eve, and Martian origin thereof. Eventually, over time, the war destroys much of the planet, and each side calls a truce, then shares resources to rebuild. I'm not sure if Earth still exists. At least it still exists in extant myths.

Comparable stories have been constructed, for instance the meteorite encased in stone in a Holy city, and religious book references about Adam and Eve. The issue with Adam and Eve stories is whether they evolved on Earth as original citizens? If not, they could have been perceived as invaders of the existing civilizations.

Then there are references to Angels and Nephilim type creatures and beings in varied religious documents. Are they, too, invaders trying to infiltrate and coerce Earth populations and other planetary system societies?

Then there are the underground source references describing beings of mythical form and societal members. Bone grubber, vomit collector, snake milker (or Krait type of snake), Resurrectionist (or body snatchers who dug up bodies or sometimes killed people to meet demand for medical research), Tosher (a scavenger who roams sewers looking for tradeable goods), Mudlark (like toshers), Plague Burier, Polewiki are chronicled in myth references. Thousands more, and thousands more in the spirit world. Specific need and particular purpose start an attempt at invocation, but a time use price must be paid regardless of service requested.

Dreams? Reality? Worlds have been told of these myths in books published, but few in those worlds spend sufficient time to discern truth from fantasy. Perhaps the few in whose memory they remain are sufficient to have influence. I suppose, in the gene pool swim, I could belong to the Shadow Souldiers. If the new Brim overlords don't possess a genetic imprint of my kin, then I don't exist, which in this new world order is a generous gift.

Perspective

Truth had become a chaos unsolvable. Only the government operated electronic connection net was authorized. All other nets were deemed anti-government, regardless of truth. Only the government truth was legal. A connection net constructed by the rebel civilizations which connected to the war-mongering civilization, like a fail-safe, existed to convince the warring civilization from destroying the rebel civilization. Use of such a net was considered treason and a reason for immediate useful disappearance.

The government was a jealous master determined to control the truth. Any non-government communication was deemed lies. Lies became truth by government edict. Truth became archaic in nature, in all science disciplines, in all legal disciplines, in all existence disciplines.

Words of any volume were not sufficient to mask a citizen from government sanction or punishment. Failure to express words upon government prompting was a crime, perceived as attempted deception. Unlawful facial expressions were viewed as signs of resistance. An improperly used facial expression in some instances could result in punishment. Citizens began to wear cloth to cover their faces as defense. The government banned facial coverings for any citizen not government sanctioned to wear one. The government workers wore masks of many fabrics and shapes as means to protect themselves from atmospheric harm which existed virtually everywhere.

It didn't take long for citizens to notice their friends and relations disappeared or died more frequently on days when use of masks were banned. Banning's were announced randomly during morning government rules pronouncements. On mask ban days, only government workers were permitted to wear masks.

Such conditions of existence affected the population unequally. Humans in the general population died or disappeared at a greater frequency. Humanoids and creature hybrids tended to show a greater resistance to atmospheric changes.

The government-built plague centers managed population health conditions. PC's, as they were known, monitored resistance to varied viruses discovered. Virus origins were never communicated to the populace. At the beginning of this post apocalypse world, many citizens visited the PC's for help. Many visitors were never seen again. The citizens began to call a PC visitor's fate "disappeared." The term evolved into a general death description across the land. The government leaders became empowered by such citizen perceptions. The citizens began to call PC's out as DC's, or death camps.

Anyone lucky enough to return from PC visits became persona non grata. Experience showed a human form devoid of purpose, as if all stamina, rigor of ethics, and reality perception had been erased in the person or hybrid being. Only close familial members of such a rebuilt type of person or hybrid being continued social contact. It was disputable whether such a reaction served existence purposefully, as casual observers couldn't know the re-appeared individual's intentions. Medically damaged? Reborn as a government spy? Example of resistance to government edict consequences? Such questions helped to consolidate government power.

The Brim world had evolved into a projection of the real world. Raised as a shield by the government. Defended in the shade by the general population. Projected as uncivilized by resistors. To not pay attention to the rulers of it attracted the overflow of an individual's tears near endless.

It could be deduced that the Brim world gave most concern to population overflows. Resources needed to survive for any length of time had reached a scarcity point. An appropriate population seemed to have not yet been calculated by the scientific crowds. Fierce resistance to the scientific groups resulted as inevitable. Trust in scientific proclamations, especially government issued, created a healthy distrust in varied population centers and social circles. Such circumstances resulted in virtual net communications wars about truth, who to believe, reality, and safety. The overlord government class could only smile. Panic was purpose. Chaos rewarding.

A corrupt government is a plague upon the land. The populace had been immunized against such thoughts, at behest and accompaniment of the corrupt government. For the government, chaos lived good, breathed good, compelled good. For citizens, chaos seemed normal over time. The slow death of morals and reason continued unabated. So many lies had been seeded into the populace, since the first day of birth, they learned little means to discern a reality feasible. Enshrined sports events, music entertainments, religious gatherings regular in nature acted as salve against such societal wounds, and also empowered the ruling government. Plans, plots, and deceits glorious became the sweet wine of the elite overlords. The lie that kept on giving.

In The Lurking

For several years, a 200-year-old pin oak tree and a 100-year-old bur ash tree had been fighting for dominion over the house. Sometimes the City and County property tax mercenaries attempted dominion also, but the owner managed to fend them off. They love money, the government overseers do, so the property owner threw it their way to rid their curse.

The waterways in life, on this planet, acted much in the same manner, as givers and takers of life in many means and forms. Sometimes persecution meant standing on the pedestal, no room available for others, and the others hate such a condition when the subjugated don't accept such a fate imposed upon them. How dare the subjugated resist their subjugators!

A gravedigger met them in the graveyard. They were looking for body parts to eat. Unholy it was, but they explained to the gravedigger they had no choice, and because of the nature of his occupation, he understood. As appreciation, they gave gravedigger some of their own detritus and advised him to burn it when he needed assistance, and their instinctual characteristics would catch the scent and make way towards gravedigger's location. For gravediggers in the Brim, this location served as a workplace and residence. He pocketed the gift.

He didn't know what to call these entities, by name. They didn't provide a name. Also, they warned him about Deacon Bone, that to trust him meant the entity of death awaited just around the corner to strike. Further, they advised Bone also recognized their aroma after a while, which could ward his entity away from transgressions planned.

They parted, and gravedigger returned to his abode nearby, a short walk away. He made a note to himself as a remembrance to bring the shovel with him while transgressing upon the cemetery grounds. His home rang only small echoes of his attempts to seek comfort. Small in grandeur, tight in space, he appreciated the simple workings of it. Almost all necessities were within easy reach.

One of those workings, his electronic net connection, served as monitor of the daily governmental chaos announcements. Humans like him took a modicum of pleasure in calling the government what is was in action and word. His appreciation for the PC and DC updates required attention. Only life and death hung on the line. It was his business to discern the lay of the land in such matters grim. His search quickly hit upon some knowledge of Deacon Bone, in written words, in videos, in pictures.

Deacon Bone uttered words of charismatic effect towards the congregation, to warn them of needed tasks ahead. To an apparently compliant crowd, he preached about tasks his minions must undertake in order to reach otherworldly salvation land. Government drones hovered above.

"It is in the demons we can't see where the most dangerous energies lay," Bone charged.

Much more of such mind mush gravedigger's brain consumed until he understood the picture Bone painted. Gravedigger stopped the search review after reading congregation responses intimating a feeling of a new awakening and the means to accomplish such a revelation. Nefarious means and methods were advocated. He clicked the off button of the machine. Started a deeper contemplation period amidst the usual aery quiet of his surroundings.

He realized most of his teeth had achieved the glorious trip heavenward before much of any other earthbound body part. His body already consisted primarily of detritus and decay patches in need of regular medicinal maintenance, as inheritance of a tragic and devastating fire conflagration at the welding rods factory where he had worked.

As security guard on that lone night, after working double shifts 3 days in a row, and one 24-hour shift, robbed of sleep, a fire of unknown origin happened. He ended up as embers, yet still alive. The recovery period acted as a season in hell for his body. As he entered an advanced recovery stage, his mind became tortured as well, particularly when looking in a full-length mirror. He had been trained to regularly do a body search during therapy, in search of removable detritus. It was painful to extricate, and gloppy medicine needed as application to stem infection of the body interior served like incantations viral. Steps needed for him to live the remainder of his time as a walking, breathing monster in appearance, although the walking illustrated a crooked and broken gate of twisted proportions. The breathing sounded out like sawed wood emanations.

His demeanor remained as lonely as usual, as the status level prior to his accident continued a similar balance to the tragic moment's aftermath. No reasonable measure of condolences or tones of solace washed away the situation from his existence. Much time alone served as comfort. repetition of his own crooked body movements. Breathing machination eventually became a comfort of sound, a melody as blind fury, of silence served in comfort. Nature sounds outside his abode windows offered a solace appreciative, as for what creatures did not exist trauma and tragedy at some point from ground to sky, and below ground and above sky depths and heights.

For him, scions of death and kin had become a measure of sustenance, for now only death ruled above him in this terrain of the Brim. Such terrain grew healthy in measure and manner at the behest of the governmental overlords. A nurse's aide in the hospital housing his body in treatment once mentioned aloud, to his surprise, "Don't miss your past. It's the past for a reason." Her meaning began to ring bells in his head, and more regularly. He wished to have listened to her wisdom once again, but soon after this alliteration, she joined the ranks of the disappeared.

Once adjusted to his new body trunk, the existence measures involved revealed a new introduction to limbs usage. The large mirror helped him to gauge limb movements up, down, side to side. Average in height among male measures, in the mirror, his new appearance portrayed to him, in reflections, as extended in length, perhaps due to a contraction in circumference.

"A stick. Nothing but a stick now." Muscle development begged attention. His medicine and new meal regiment helped to restore and maintain a subtle decency. His eyes, at least the usable remainders, begged a tortuous amount of energy to adjust on any particular general object appearance, and impossible to gauge details presentation. The windows to his soul healed shattered, but still usable.

His appearance pushed him towards another part of society, the part once deemed unsociable. He worked to become acquainted with the societal monsters. They philosophized much, told each other stories of sustenance, breaker of hearts sonnets, orchestrations of killed desires.

Ultimately, to a degree, these commiserations allowed them an agreement on a theory of contiguous social circles in which they resided. A point, where they lived, encircled by comfort zones of abode and immediate environs, but in the adjacent circle, dots of harm existed, navigated by all who transgressed in that circle phase. Each circle entered another phase of fortune and solitude, or disaster and pain. The final destination remained a mystery, as many government disappeared. At least, such rumors prevailed perhaps driven by panic or unfortunate pause moments of rumination. Government reported death statistics, but not many still in the living world cared or believed any longer a recitation of numbers presented by the overlord entities.

They "crumbs", as they sometimes referred to themselves, did eventually get into a verbal argument, calmed down, then again an argument escalated. The meetings began to take an ugly turn. Rumors ruled that scene.

"Don't eat the soup."

"There's not much else to eat."

"Why do you think we were moved to the soup district?"

"I heard from someone who knew a soup factory worker and he said the soup is funny."

The banter ensued about whether the soup provided necessary sustenance, or had been hashed into a slow poisoning substance. Disappearance has become more than common at present. Paranoia lurked as the next level of mind disease, just a smidge below government's daily pronouncements.

Some meeting events devolved into a physical wrestling match, which seemed to stimulate some in the group, while the flesh detritus flew in waves. Eventually some of the group copulated in all manners and means, then relaxed, as if in reality, their minds required such an energy release to ward of death's cleaver and achieve a mental state of repose. sometimes more animal creature in manner and tone than humanoid, but these moments helped them to better explore and adjust to the current bodily conditions imposed upon them by life experiences.

Sometimes actions commenced as a buoy for another's safety, sometimes mimicked sharks in search of food emotional swimming towards each other.

Gravedigger's mind ventured into a cloudy, random memory journey into a time when his lover told him not to say, "I love you." It was yet too much of a psyche burden. He verbally offered they could practice, practice love, and the entanglements involved in and during the process. She seemed quite stunned and somewhat angry in her visual appearance, in response. She stated she didn't want to experience it again, at least not now, as the breaking of it, the feeling of love in the past, almost exhausted her of life. He relented to her desire, expressed an understanding tone of meaning. This life may be going everywhere but anywhere but it lived as a last bit of resort, he thought.

Their one time of love itself making, and not just thoughts or dreams of love, but the ingredients physical of love seasoned by passion, she relented and tried, but still looked away at the finish, the climax, as if residing in significant contemplation moments while he repeatedly espoused his love during orgasm. Love by sweat ensued, accompanied by tear's showers, joint pains, skin tingles and rips, and flushed tones, follicles of hairs disheveled all along the stems forward, back and swayed wild., at the moment of no rhyme or reason. Ejaculation evident for him exhibited by groans horrible, wild, creepy, and yet she, still silent in a dream as the actor in a picture show moving but devoid of sound. Creme de la creme from beginning to end. Rickety hearts beat in tandem as a sign, separate of skin and bone sharing, of almost a community of two souls, as the semblance of beauty heaved forth a last breath. Each had allowed some taking of each other in the mix of flesh and tissue. Juliet had not betrayed Romeo, just had stepped back in mind for further rumination. Only now contemplation ruled the stained sheets of wrinkled plains. Love postponed, only delayed. Love making yet the bridge to breach.

Love evolved from actions repetitive, until such repetitions acted as signals for action or otherwise. No one had a right, or a demand, to another being's sympathy. For some, love resided only between the lower appendages. Give out a pull, or a rub. Maybe it will be reciprocated in kind. Make a deposit into the hope chest. Contribute to the VD fund. Secret Saint Nick awaits. The worser angels of his nature had alighted upon his mind. A world devoid of magic glows like a miasma of lonely quiet. A world devoid of love existed as a world lost. Love fell to second in the list right behind survival.

In the medical case of each, their minds had become rewired, almost reverted to a more animal instinct stage, uncontrollable in form and fashion to an everyday humanoid. They plotted imaginary hunts and what they might do for food if necessary, to the body of the human, humanoid, or hybrid creature. These developments instinctually scared them in degrees. They didn't desire a life as hunted targets of other living things.

Maybe the gods don't have the power to kill us when they want to. Maybe they try, but if failure results, we are pushed down the death queue as their need to satisfy in the distant future. They made us sentient for a reason, he suspected. Perhaps higher beings figured, well, the Brimmers will sort it out. We did. The plan is simple chaos, and all that scheme encumbers.

Always lurked in the shadows an army, or posse of ill-disposed in nature ready to take down a notch or two those of whom they wanted to punish for hard earned successes they themselves had failed to achieve. Just the juice they were of necessity's ring. No justice or decency entered into that mixing bowl. Justice and decency had been outlawed on unpredictable days of government pronouncements. Chaos organized chaos.

The crumbs community wished further counsel about their current existence conditions, in the abodes allowable to inhabit, but had sought alone silence so much, the thought of humanoid interaction caused anxiety strong in each. They determined to continue observe and listen, as humanoids conversed outside their abode, on the streets, sidewalks, during chance and planned encounters. Listened to conversations, observed mannerisms. and too the wild creatures they spied, for similar activity exhibits, from bugs and insects at ground level and through the air, and birds, bees, wasps, rabbits, squirrels, foxes, snakes, spiders. No need to bring flowers anymore to funerals or burial ceremonies. The flowers died out first.

Deacon Bone's mysticism began to reign supreme over the crumbs' lands. So, as defense, they developed a strategy to mimic and practice the activities of sound and motion humans and hybrid creatures displayed. Comical and tragic at the same time these plays proceeded on the living room floor stage, after furniture moved to allow such activity. Along this way, their sexual instincts, still intact, overtook the stage at times. They were unable to resist such moments, as the instincts overtook them during these time periods. Afterwards, they wondered if any other instincts might become aroused in them. It was during these conversation and cohabitation moments when the macabre entered communication modes. Such discussions regularly devolved into morbid actions and attractions now seemingly inbred into their crooked anatomies and broken brain parts.

This place in the Brim land reads bleak. Long ago the land died, refused to give new life absent significant prodding, and the sea lay deader. No one, human, humanoid, or creature hybrid goes to the poisoned seas, and all life forms tolerate the remaining land conditions for survival. The skies provide a flicker of light mostly shrouded by mysteries of fog unwilling to reveal secrets, yet the fog drops moisture enough, rare and useable to sustain life still.

Our most concerning issue remained the Deacon. Some of us had spied on the meetings promenaded over by Deacon Bone. His acolytes appeared happy, but a closer look at their faces revealed a dead stare, as if a smile had been painted upon the facial lips. The immediate measure of safe existence resided in the workings of the fighting Deacon Bone and his army.

Gravedigger received word of a commotion rising in the distance as the cemetery guard spirits alerted him to invasion. In somber tones they advised the female in his life had been killed among many others. They were not certain whether she had resurrected as one of Bones minions. Gravedigger certainly wished not, as he didn't want the responsibility of dispatching her. The spirits asked him to hold back, secure himself in his abode, until he was dispatched further. He remained alone with his memories of a love he hoped to coax further towards a joining of their spirits not empoisoned by Bone's magic.

The spirits and ghoul allies waged a noisy battle against Bone's forces. Each thirsted for each other, reluctantly, but out of survival necessity. Control of these grounds reached critical for survival amongst each group. Gravedigger didn't know the identity of the cemetery spirit group leader.

The fight seemed lost, based on his interpretation of the sound and fury of the outside struggle. Loud echoes of grave monuments and markers plunking into the ground caused a shudder in him. The spirits would not have moved these objects except as a last resort.

His mind remained lost on this issue, but then he searched deep inside for strength, tapped into memories of his lost love, and the pains of his injury and recovery status. He realized the shovel in his hand, but did not recall picking it up for the floor. He lost sight of reality, as he flickered like a dying light bulb on last sparks.

He drew strength from these passion and painful memorials; drew forth energies throughout his body, searching for the vigor needed to jump high, almost fly, and swing his limbs back and forth, imposing a killing impact upon the foes. Before realizing it, his body existed whole in the fray and fought madness. With each desiccation of an evil dead, more strength absorbed into his body lifting the veil of horrors.

Even when landing jumps his mind zeroed in on kills. Swatches of death and flying limbs forced Deacon Bone to take notice. Gravedigger moved towards Bone, struck the near-fatal blow, then watched a repetitive chaos of body blows upon limbs, trunks all around until the horrid eventual finish. Gravedigger's pre-set trap readied, Bone fell to ground into it, allowing the sacred ground to suck down and cave in upon him, and crush out of him spirit, will, and life.

Fatally injured detritus creatures crawled toward their mates, caressed the respective remains knowing one day resurrection would beckon in times of need to avenge any future planned indiscretions attempted against their kin. Gravedigger, previously desecrated and returned to the top portion of cemetery ground, saw beauty in the fate they had taunted towards themselves. Beautiful the moment streamed into his eyes, despite torn and tattered perspective. The scent of his loved one's hair and eyes enveloped him. He inhaled it over and over again. His compatriots then completed expiration on top of each other in varied plains of the cemetery grounds, as mutual shields prepared for the travel into the next life.

Exhausted just in the watching of these scenes, he spied and found a place to sit and rest his crooked bones. He had taken enough for this day in the world of Brim. Misery regular strolled certain as another moment in this place. Some solace could be taken in knowing misery ends, life begins again, as broken usual, but peaceful for a time. Endarked as this place had become, he could still consider it home.

On the walk back to his abode, he encountered a demon creature, or so he deduced, much like him, in the gender apposite his. They agreed to become friends after unsteadying self-introductions, but each had reached the end of the task. Agreed to co-habit, and philosophize wild, woolly, and merry about varied creature and humanoid events particular to their residence, neighborhood, greater community, and larger world sphere.

The seasons will have their way now, measuring time and truth. Winter, when silence speaks softly. Spring, when fairy wings sing a dance. Summer, when crickets burp a mystical chirp. Autumn, when cool breezes and winds blanket the skin.

Present Time Revisit

Perhaps we citizens shouldn't have allowed the devolvement of our country to the point of poorly elected politicians mandating us, literally, into death. I'm a seat of the pants traveler. every moment, including walking path steps and up to car, bus, train, plane rides imposes morbid scenes and evokes fears of horrid injury or death. If I wrote all of it down I'd fill a volume at least as large as an encyclopedia volume. I can't make that fly, or I'd literally knock myself out. After writing periods, I sometimes sleep on and off for days punctured by cat naps or sloth periods where dreams then invade and torture my mind.

Another foreshadowing of great aunt Helen's has captured my mind, so I let it travel to the unknown destinations, like the Brim itself. Sure, it's the writer's life for me, as it has been from a young age, but the slog sometimes accumulated too much dust and detritus, feels like the size of a planetoid. and so there my mind rests, watching, waiting for the next adventure to invade my mind, as I watch the characters evolve into creatures of one form or another, then enter the escapades of the story.

As a midnight trancer the thoughts are sparked to life, begin an evolution. Who is the creature who stalks my mind? The goal of the creature seems to be to trip up the prey, cause it to injure itself through fear errors, bumps, falls from body motion like runs, lurches, movements errant. Then, it takes the victims souls.

Tree limb tapping window. Blown by wind? Squirrels, no, nighttime when they rest. Raccoon, too high from ground level. Rats in the walls? Memories. Must be memories, but in what kind of physical form?

What gets in? Sight of shadow, smell of unknown origin. Immediate death has not smell, so a living organism it must be. Memories of all sensations except smell when music played. Real memories or song memories sparking real memories. Memories were as dependable as a cup of coffee or tea prepared by someone else. The else always asserted itself, even in the fast-food places. Well, not always. Nothing was always.

What tries to leave? Memories, sensations past, reaper harvest and he to become harvested? What's worse? Drowning in tears or drowning in the ocean. Each circumstance is a lonely horror. Each one is potentially dangerous and deadly.

I now see myself as if in a dream. I am him, he imagined.

Himself he saw caught webbed. Where's the exit, for him? For it? What am I? Don't need to be sucked into the philosophy death pit, generously full of thought kernels, genuinely bereft of reality accuracy.

Memories or murmurs. "I'll be going to my grave as my last thoughts strum the sounds of your mom sucking my dick." He's a pinball being played, ejected forth, shaken into and out of tight spots, avoiding the dark expiation depths beyond the red flippers. "I don't even know your mom," he squelched out, as last words of a condemned soul. Time for a new, hot, breathing cup of coffee, or tea.

All connected, these thoughts. I attempted a view of the being resident in this body, only one present, along with many personalities developed over a long year.

What's it he calls it. Gets into his mind, he only imagines it entering his body, but thinks of it as an actual entry. Still trying to figure out such a configuration of fate. Perhaps a survival mechanism taking over as necessary. It's just life. It's just Brim.

As he creeps around to discover the uninvited guest's attempt to enter him, then enter and mooch around, then try to leave, he rummages through his own personal failures and tragedies, and also reads out medications prescribed to him, to illustrate personality changes.

He was inhabited by the kind of brain that felt comfortable in an industrial setting. The whir of exhaust fans, clink of metal to metal, scratches of pigeons and bats attempting entry into the warehouse of finished goods. Music floated into his soul, played for his soul, massaged his soul. He was unable to corral the thoughts, to block them, kept him from falling into those happy times. Happy times tended to mask imminent dangers, he'd learned long ago, or he believed he had done so.

His body shook, shivered, but still relaxed from the memory massage. Time for the dreams of day and night to die. All light is gray now, and so too, all dark. No dividing line presents itself for certain. The urgency for continued life beckons.

Always and forever autumn it seems like a patchwork of souls encircles this plain. The Brim overlords own those plains, and so too, him and anyone who inhabits them. Seized control over everyone and every resource. Independent thoughts outlawed and punished. Freedom is slavery, they banter about in printed words and espoused beacon announcements. Slavery is freedom.

This Brim is the home world of all things in it. A roving planet, in transition and transaction, from old ways to new ways of existence experimentation, has limited resources which are scavenged from nearby planetoid orbs.

Professional mobs of people are paid by controlling government to spread propaganda for citizen mind control. The population is becoming dumbed down because the gene pool distribution is government controlled to achieve such effects. Any independent innovation is banned, subject to a death penalty, as only the government is allowed to innovate.

Of course, if independent innovations are discovered, they are immediately ceased, seized, and once in government possession, studied for utility value. If deemed adequate, then propaganda is released announcing this new government discovery. The individual responsible for the innovation or invention is imprisoned, stowed away for future governmental use. While imprisoned, the genes are stolen from an inventor's anatomy, then the innovator eventually disappears, and the gene pool is upgraded by injecting the genes into a female host who brings the resulting embryo to term, upon which time the government raises it in a home and school environment. These new babies are called "braces" because they will become the bedrock of a new civilization. Humans are essentially planet food. Their existence is subject to nature's needs and whims. Humans might resist such notions, but nature doesn't care. Sometimes happiness flees from us like a feral cat. Like a feral feline, sometimes happiness flees.

Since the beginning of human sentience, outlawing evil has never been a terribly effective method of eliminating it. Outlawing the means to protect against evil is certainly a path to a life of hell. Politicians tend to forget, shielded by their own castle wall arrogance, that we trusted them with our toils and money. If they break their promises, we will pick up the broken pieces and shove them back up their arses, and move on.

Humanoids are as predictable in some ways, as nature, according to the human authored Field Guide. The mouse has become larger and more viral through ignorance of such human constructs. For some, dominion over the entire planet remains too small for practices of their wiles. And for some, a jail cell sized space is sufficient. "Seek a conjunction of the middle space called in-between," reads as wisdom in the humanoid Field Guide about humans. Just a patchwork of souls, like a wart on the body politic.

Despite all human created technological advances, they remain domiciled as subjects to the tender mercies of nature. Human created technology companies conspire with corrupt governments. Hires thieves to steal or break technology on a regular basis in order to enhance sales and riches. Some examples include pipeline construction, energy resources control, technology development, political party money laundering as a business entity unto itself. Political parties hired pave the way for such exploitation moral or devious by creating written rules, enforcing them with banshee vigor against designated enemies, but mainly against political competitors, the worker classes, and political classes out of favor; uses big media to brainwash the worker classes. All swirling in the conspiracy pool to make poorer and more dependent the designated lesser classes as part of the grand plan.

The labeled elites can make anything, any action, any purchase illegal, even in hindsight (hindsight laws) and sic hounds of hell upon the workers. They can target citizens for destruction using communication tech and machines. The machines serve as a booby trap to ask questions about society, then track responses for signs of non-government sponsored misinformation. They are the jealous nitpicking never-do-wells bent on destruction of communities who resist the technology and politician monopolies over existence.

As a means to control the population expansion beyond mere stability, a published government rule of existence stated: Keep the baby, abort the mother. The population ignored it as if it were a mistake, but no retraction was issued.

Wake Up When The Dead Sleep

Time passed. Evening turned to morning. Morning Time passed. Evening turned into morning. Morning didn't care how much sleep needed, or knew about fears or phobias. Another day in the Brim had been granted. Another day of life bestowed. Maybe the dead could sleep in peace for a while. Tired eyes can't see much clear. Tired minds could only see darkness a bit clearer. In this new world of permanent gray, sounds had become clues to some hope, some life.

Hope offered many avenues for the mind to travel. Lost ones, disappeared ones, memories of each still lived in the minds granted hope. The hot razors in my heart are a weapon. Tears healed. I can no longer see loving eyes, except in sleep. The color of my dreams are misty blue.

The government doesn't give a rat's ass bout you. Decent people protests failed. Death for liberty failed. Only the government and criminals can now acquire and point guns. We're two shits away from an overflowed toilet. No one wants to admit depression is stoked by suffering moments unavoidable, and avoiding moments experience needed. Humans are utterly and completely groomed to become stupid fools. We are more compliant servants to those who teach us, and the governments they serve. We bow to authority as a means to survive the rigors placed upon us. "Government, I'm home!"

But the government didn't want us in a home comfortable. The abyss in me deepened. My idea to defeat enemies is to convince them to defeat themselves. Internal rot run amuck. The people seek success most of their lives, but along the way sell out to slavish fictions of reality until they retire and are set free. As I've grown in age, I began to realize the chaos of others is no longer my forest of sorrows. The government, on the other hand, wants to punish us for not living their lies properly.

Trust your innate instincts. You have but one body to survive in, according to my Aunt Helen.

"May the sun warm your mind. May the moon cool your spirit." That saying she coined to help me to remember often forgotten blessing. She almost sang the words in a soothing rhythm. We shared each other's time. We learned from each other. Another gem she espoused as, "There's bears, bulls, and foxes. Everyone ignores the foxes." Her way of reminding me trust is earned and not granted.

Still more wisdom I recalled under her teaching influences. "There's a reason for everything. Some reasons remain a mystery. There's a reason they are undiscoverable." She promised me one day I may see the sun again. She knew it was there from her book reading. No one of her generation or the one previous had ever felt it, but for a slight warmth on days when the clouds finished crying on her. From the stoop outside the summer kitchen door she would point up and imagine it, saying, "It's called the sun.

Apparently it doesn't like much attention because if you look at it too long it will sting your eyes into darkness blind."

One day I heard her talking to a neighbor outside and they talked about a new love life matter a few housing blocks away. I wondered what was love. What did it feel like. When she came back into the house, and saw my confused look, she realized I heard something of the conversation. Her intuition, strong as always, somewhat mocked a perspective. She laughed and said, "Love is the longest prison sentence, even if it only lasts for a minute."

Years later, when the first sting of love struck my heart, I understood. I thought about what the effect would have. Distracts, deceiving. She offered more advice at that time. "Learn how to follow your own heart before you follow others." She later counseled me that I must learn about passions and reactions to moments. Control passions or lose yourself in rage. A person can't follow themselves if they lose control. "Reacting to false impulse. Those impulses will trick you like fairies at mischief." I asked, "Like the garden sprites?" She nodded in a yes fashion.

The Wedding

It is the day and time of virulent copulation among the sexes and genders. Some of each group succumbs to the government poisons spread in the fog, once trapped in government regulated zones. They are advertised as safe zones, but they are designed as traps to ensnare a populace viewed as zombies despite no such creature catalogued as sentient on the Brim planetoid.

The party is on. Holy communion XXX of dead flesh and living soul. A music fest, a dance palooza, a flesh feast of rigor to the death from exhaustion. Nonsensical it seems, until it is understood one more day seems eternal like in time. No sun shines to ring the chimes of day. No pipe organs sound out somber classical tones of repose.

Humans, humanoids, hybrid-creatures many as yet uncatalogued in the species journals joined for an anticipated last day when their use becomes evidence of a value only the government can measure. Allowance to live one more day. Needed in a battle of living humanoids vs. the dead vs. gargoyles (rumored) vs. shapeshifter ghouls. No winners, no losers, just piles and piles of deadened spirits. An elaborate means of control, pleasure's served. As the last moments of grief-stricken and torn flesh moans emoted upon the landscape, a small laugh became a larger and larger laugh from the voice of Deacon Bone worshippers, still extant upon the landscape in random clans amidst the Brim. Extant to still poison minds in unwary circles and circumstances of humanoid habitation.

His preached sermons still slipped form worshipper's lips in song tones.

"Finally, my work is done."

They cupped their hands to each ear. Awaited the final silence. It arrived unmerciful.

"And now I'm bored."

The wanted some chips and dip, but no servants were available, yet, to serve them.

"Was that a bird's chirp? Mourning dove or night raven?"

The Deacon's words still haunted his followers, in joy, in mourning, as broken souls moored to a post unbreakable.

The Rausch State

The control system for the populace remained a curious mystery. The leader's name as mentioned previously wasn't frequently uttered as the soldiers, sometimes called monitors of the system didn't name their actions or purpose as deemed necessary in the leader's name. Speculation of the populace centered on secrecy as protection. They knew such a life of secrecy also offered some protection to themselves and their small communities. Communities remained small because of the persecution of large communities, known as regularly raided by Davosian troopers. Why the raids happened remains a mystery, perhaps to keep the populace unaware of a means to avoid or sidestep them through word or deed. All living creatures could be marked for disappearance.

What resulted in the population's mind was a Rausche effect, or a flow state of effortless effort, also referred to as a dizzying sort of ecstasy. The concept had been passed on from another world, and the term Rausche coined by someone named Goethe. Whether he, she, or it, no certainty existed regarding Goethe's occupation. Philosopher? Painter? Author? Scientist? Psychologist? Such credentials identification became coffee and cookie, or tea and biscuit talk.

Would there be three critical human or humanoid states necessary for such a level of existence. First, body (includes brain or CPU); second, spirit (includes personality); third, soul (engine force). Robots could be programmed to exist in a flow state. Historical records revealed robots worked on Mars, Earth, and gradually became constructed to emulate a human and humanoid appearance. The robot hearts worked from batteries. They worked primarily on outer space missions. A confusing issue remained whether all living creatures were robots.

Most species had developed an ability to replicate lost or damaged parts. Virtually every living creature could be categorized as robot in form and function including an expiration date. Living conditions promoted a functional continuation beyond expiration dates. Interactions with environment and social situations could terminate function ability, but resurrections through reconstruction happened regularly if cost-effective.

Resurrection served as a self-replicating ability. Memories and learning could be transferred from each generation to the next. Knowledge accumulation serves a useful purpose for future generations. Deviant purposes could also ensue.

Societal evolution could become altered. First they attack the big brains on the planets or planetoids. Proceed to program the leaders mentally to start the assault, which results in large technical innovations like the internet, then mobile phones, then space discovery mechanisms which improves technical object development, then brain washes the humans and humanoids known species gene pool. Super accumulations of knowledge could be computer programmed for faster evolution purposes. Leaders and those wealthy to afford such conversions could afford the costs to change their own brains and bodies into biotech designed, god-like entities.

The end stage is where all universe civilizations could wage wars for control of the most resources. Solar system battles, galaxy battles, and more. All of the survivors who failed to be converted would potentially serve as slaves to the ruling orthodoxy group, or become disappeared, or terminated if their parts were deemed no longer recyclable.

The powerful, patrons, and puppets would remain the only remaining classifications of usefulness. Subsets of these classifications could exist. A heightened level of sentience is not immune from desires scurrilous or banal. If emotions were not programmed out of the gene pool, then pleasures of mind, body, and soul wouldn't disappear. Such mindsets would still exist to plague continuation of an efficient civilization. Harmony and chaos would still dance the dance.

For instance, hypnosis is a mind control psychological contraption. Essentially, mind control. Tech control can alter our dreams, mold our imaginations, stimulate physical actions, personality, create harmony or chaos, like in a tech war game, or games designed to emulate civilization building. Still, such games could become designed to trick the user into false realities of devious merit. These games and diversions develop the human mind and physical interaction capabilities, but also break down the consciousness state into one that evolves into a near permanent sub-conscious state in which the designers could exploit for ultimate and near sole control. Game players thus became test subjects for war games, survival games, and more.

Once the flow state concept took hold, governments exploited it into varied resource assets. Robots, cyborgs, were in effect created as a trans humanoid species where humans on solar system objects like moons, planets, planetoids used them for essential service's needs. Learn about it, erase from mind the foreground noise of nature, humanoids, planet geology, in order to discover the universal flow state, and who controls it. The "who" in control used the mystery of their societal composition to hide from any potential responsibility for failures, much like management communities in any factory, corporation, or government entity.

The Rausche philosophy then explored the society subjugated to find any other species to exploit, and spread like disease the concept across all communities. Excuses for such a need of Rausche acceptance where emitted by media and tech companies everywhere until the governed provinces and regions of all sentient civilizations passively consented. The governments regularly created distractions of petty themed laws and regulations to swirl minds too busy looking for a next meal and protective shelter to any longer notice or care or question.

This entire universe could exist solely as a test game for a civilization of higher sentient thought and knowledge. Why our game participation is needed remains a mystery. A deduction might be that chaos and confusion makes compliant the citizen minds. Any complaints registered during the process disappeared into the miasma of the government behemoth, so much so that citizens would relent to the subjugation methods they could see with their own eyes. Acclimation by defeat spread everywhere.

What They Do In The Dark

Citizens evolved in mindsets and physicality over eons as means to survive in the Rausche states formed. A key to preventing a meshing of the mindsets remained in segregation of the civilizations through communication monitoring. Some in the present time in the Brim surmised poor communication availability to be an intentional government mechanism necessary in their world since adequate communication could be exploited to harness the rising tide of living conditions complaints. Rumors did spread of uprisings, and the most prevalent gossip concerned what happened at a well-known wealthy

Estate land, the location of which no one could name specifically.

Workers at the Estate had gradually evolved into creature forms whether by nature's way or by research at the land location. The creatures were nature-created hybrids of known and undocumented animal and humanoid sentients, used to going about the house, cleaning it of spirits, demons, and other bumps in the night. Inexplicably, rats, mice, squirrels, spiders were prohibited to clean, and allowed to roam about randomly. The cleaning purpose ordered by Estate owners involved hunting after extant creatures which undermined the owners' daytime works.

During implementation of the Estate owners' instructions a hybrid creature made of stone, parchment, dagger was discovered. Not only a hybridization process emerged, but a process of inanimate objects formulation. Further unusual, this hybrid type exuded a living, movable form capable of engagement in small and minute household tasks. Stones flung forth on command like bullets, although accuracy in target hitting remained an issue. Some of the hybrid types created harm such as skin burns. Parchment elements of the hybrids branded tattoos in many walls, objects, and the creature workers' body parts, as if commanded to do so. Daggers cut slim and deep.

Commands to initiate such actions weren't audible, as if the objects had developed their own minds and instincts. Eventually, the animate objects escaped, were never found, and infiltrated the populated centers acting in the same manner as rats, mice, squirrels, and spiders, which now remained scarce in sight, perhaps hiding, conceding territorial haunts, then found other land areas more secretive.

The strangest aspect of the little hybrids existence involved stories from current Brim residents, voiced during social events. The stories concerned instances of kitchen utensils and objects, and outdoor landscaping implements coming to life, sometimes to rescue a resident of the location from imminent harm or accident. The incidents where attributed to spirits and ghosts, perhaps demons, too. An ending to a recited instance tale usually rung out as good fortune or a guardian angel appearance, but in some cases, small to significant harm resulted. Speculation circled wild about harm incidents, particularly regarding the exposed potential guilt of the harmed entity, as if the harm were a warning or execution of a spell by a competitor or someone who had felt harmed and sought retribution. The range of travel radius for the living inanimate objects remained unknown.

Any such society as the Brim inhabitants could be accused of living as paranoids, fearful of all around them in this world. In the Brim, paranoia feelings and sentiments seemed warranted as a survival mechanism fueled by stresses of an uncertain existence quotient. I wondered sometimes if a fear meter should be placed around in public places. Residents could gauge whether a fearful appearance in the area proved a valid defense mechanism. Fear all or fear nothing seemed irrational and dangerous. A healthy fear allowed retreat from many forms of predators in nature and government.

We learned through generations of existence that fear of government inspectors was a purposeful reaction. Most always their appearance meant intelligence gathering was underway. We spied on those who spoke to the inspectors. Instances of inspectors infiltrating the population remained uncommon, but perhaps these brief meeting instances were so well masked in effort, we were unable to reliably target a suspect.

Some citizens lived alone, rarely seen, even at social meetings and impromptu gatherings. Some were raised to treat alone as safe. Misplaced or misspoken words could ruin the individual or that individual's family and friends. Once a person was designated as an enemy of the overlords, the government considered such a seed as weed spread. Fumigation commenced.

Earworms developed, became difficult to extract, after repetitive and daily government pronouncements infected the minds of the populace like music sounds stuck in a loop. The pronouncements swirled in minds on a regular basis, remained unescapable. When I discovered this portion of the Brim world on my travels for edible food and usable shelter, the government sounds could not escape my attention whether wide awake, tired, or as echoes during sleep. The circumstances helped me to avoid survival memories.

My prior encounters with government inspectors resulted in a brief episode of internment at a facility mysterious. Most of the time I was injected to cause a hypnotic fuzzy mind function in me. The experimentations perpetrated upon me, I discovered, sometimes by accident, abilities genetically altered during the times I was used as a test subject entity. Healing qualities and the ability to use portions of non-injured body parts to repair injured body parts, I discovered randomly. The uninjured parts I transferred, particularly skin and ligament tissue, would grow back quickly.

Eventually, during rest and rumination periods of my travels, I learned to replace the used parts for needed bodily injury repairs. Recently deceased animals, hybrid creatures, humanoids, and other humans also worked as viable replacement parts. To trigger the replacement process effectiveness, I only needed to think or wish the healing for it to occur once the replacement parts were applied. I became rather adept at the process over time. Not sure if these replacement became part of my anatomy permanently. I appear mostly human when fully clothed. My body hair has grown longer in some places, serves to keep me warm and dry during cold, windy, or rainy days.

I don't honestly recall being released from the facility where I was housed. The last moment I can remember from the incident is when I looked back to measure my walk direction and noted the facility, but it looked antiquated and unused for some time. I've suffered hallucinations randomly. The usual conditions of reality sometimes seem difficult to perceive.

I'm able to experience what I'm doing, but also able to see myself doing it as if some type of perspective sense has been enhanced in present time. A bit confusing to understand, but the experience of it has become less fuzzy as if the environment around me exists as dreamscape and not entirely foot over soil landscape. Guessing this ability was turned on during my internment at the government research facility. Was my purpose there to be converted into a government weapon? Need more info. The earworms played with my mind.

What is an earworm song purpose? I seemed to now know something about their effects and influences. I may have been programmed to follow government mandates as an example to citizens about how to follow the Brim land rules. Only three paths seemed logical and reasonable to serve the overlord's needs.

Sexual experimentation, but masturbation is only sometimes allowed for imagination constructions and physical relief, as if ejaculation removed microscopic wastes. Essentially served as a mind cleansing mechanism. Intercourse with other beings could provide biological and genetic historical results for evaluation of progeny produced. Progeny stronger in mind and body and spirit in some respects, or weaker, or more compliant were possibilities.

Must only eat foods allotted. Food appeared, in boxes and bins, outside the neighborhood living blocks, accessible by the use of DNA prints. To open the box, just had to press a part of the outer skin against the box. If it didn't open, it wasn't meant for the person trying to open it. Each box provided enough food sources for about a week. Tasted a bit like old newspaper at times, but nutritional needs were served. Attempts to eat any food sources other than the boxed foods was rumored to cause severe illness and incapacitation, sometimes death.

Sometimes whole families didn't receive food drops. Sharing was outlawed, but sharing regularly happened. Government tracker Agents would sometimes flock to areas when sharing happened. Citizens would then begin to disappear at varied intervals. We began to consider whether the boxed foods contained microscopic tracking devices. At social meetings, the issue was debated, heatedly at times. These debates were dangerous to undertake. Use of incorrect words or word combinations could result in disappearance.

Entertainment avenues and issues also stimulated the government's interest. There were no significantly audible music sounds in this world, just dings and dongs that denoted permitted socializing locations and activities, and the scheduled times they were authorized. Making unauthorized sounds became a crime punishable by imprisonment or disappearance. The government deemed some citizens sounds were coded to plot shenanigans unauthorized. To determine an unlawful coding system became tricky. Populations in some areas had developed alternative means to sing, such as during sexual activity when emotional sounds could be voiced in varied tones, pitches, and frequency. Or while walking during permitted times amidst the allowed landscapes, blending steps and clothing swishes, and limb movements to mimic musical expression.

Discovery of my life existence purpose as a programmed governmental experiment entity seemed impossible. Much thinking I progressed upon. If we are made in the image of our creators, then some of our skills and abilities likely mimic theirs. The appearance of the body housing the ultimate leader likely is similar to ours. Leaders tend to be pathological narcissists who would revel over copies similar yet subservient to their inner and outer selves. It is the greatest weakness of an intelligent such personality. Progeny embracing. Mirror preening. The oppressor's favored pastime. What to do about it if anything? Damn the flow state, or take the easy drift? I contemplated.

Found I possess physical powers, activated by emotions. Stronger bones. Increased flexibility. I can jump higher, climb anything like an acrobat, enter a stealth mode physically where the body blends skin color and even changes the color of clothing threads to match the scenery around me, like an animal creature in the wild. Enhanced night vision. Essentially, re-bred to become a government soldier for the purpose of crowd control and punishment if required, to keep citizens in line. My mind still contemplated life from a Shadow Souldier perspective.

Ridiculous Ruminations Reasonable

We lived in different neighborhoods based on intelligence, ethnicity, and programed to live certain ways. Personal and private rights were not a choice as the government determined all without the consent of citizens. Examples of a planned insanity revealed themselves gradually.

Work at job assigned, go home, entertain self in the proscribed ways, serious crime to do otherwise. Death penalty only for unauthorized sexual activity, as lesser classes were guinea pigs for use by the elites. A few nights a week , and a few daytimes a month allotted for greater entertainment allotments, depending on work production.

The entire system revolved around who could cheat themselves into the best benefits allotted. If caught, the perpetrator disappeared for unknown reasons, whether promoted or demoted is uncertain. Demotion was rumored to involve supervised experimentations conducted by government authorized overseers, such as operational experimentation on any part of the subjects body, including sometimes removal or rearrangement of body parts.

Who actually ruled and how the government system operated had a consistency of glitches and mystery that defied known and experienced facts. Much marketing and commercialism used to create societal interests and expectations, all coordinated by the government entities in charge. The governmental system of laws implementation and procedures also varied. Such information we obtained from infrequent visitors of varied species. Still difficult to determine if the visitors were government paid infiltrators or innocents escaping persecution or disappearance circumstances.

Varied population controls existed differently for select parts of the Brim lands. Sex days granted, but had to be earned. Partners chosen by government allotment. Procreation is only allowed through an earned permit authorized by the government. Partners could be human, humanoid, or creature hybrids. Interbreeding across species permitted.

I was arrested one day, and the he of me could see the circumstance coming, but my powered abilities somewhat emboldened me to trade capture for further government induced illumination. The arrest involved unauthorized sexual activity, but he knew he had not violated any laws, rules, or customs. Jailed, then prosecuted, but during the prosecution, one question irritated me. I'm not sure why.

"You are resistant to our edification efforts," the prosecutor mocked.

"I'm hungry," he responded.

Then a loud click popped into the attention of everyone in the courtroom except him. All of the people in the room began coughing and itching eyes and body parts randomly, then seemed to die, after faintly visible gas he could see and smell pumped into the room, except he didn't die. Just fainted, then woke up in a factory that processed lifeless bodies.

Since his body was considered dead, he was about to be processed into reusable parts by a machine, when he awoke, and rolled off the rolling chain line, then onto some metal girders that entangled him. Converted himself to present immediate perspective. I escaped and then looked for a place to hide until the time to figure out what to do. After contemplating, reverted to the "he" perspective for better reconnaissance ability and information collection.

He met a person he thought recognizable while hiding. It was a neighbor friend who lived a few doors down from his blocked living space, but the friend had changed. He looked more like a primitive man than modern human. The man's mind was nearly blank of thought. An ability to form words seemed difficult. The man ranted randomly at times. Scared him.

He asked the man what happened. Story recitation ensued. The man went on a brief walk journey and showed what had happened. His body was captured at night, then moved to a different housing block where people had been changed into a body similar in look, texture, and verbalization as his being had been changed into. He applied current perspective for additional feedback. I guessed through genetic tampering, but didn't reveal the thought.

Apparently the government was trying to create a smarter, stronger humanoid, and used lower classed humans to experiment upon. All of them were essentially locked up in the block housing towns and cities to be used as experimental entities when necessary. A familiar ring tone sounded in me.

I was seated at a table. Across from me sat an old man in appearance. My senses streamed not all man, but also, part creature. One I had never seen before, or smelled. I wondered what next. The place exuded an eerie aura.

"Inanimates," the old man said, then added, "they are animate."

"Oh. Didn't mean to agitate them," I responded. The cabinets jiggled a leery quake.

"Just a sec," the old man growled out, much like the noise of a coyote, but a bit lower in tone. "Sometimes I don't know when the joints might give out, like the connection is temporarily lost."

I attempted to ingest his meaning. Uh, there it is. The old man creature lifted a thin lit cigar lodged between his fingers. A smoke lifted from the cigar tip, now shortened in stature by repeated oral huffs in, and exhaled slowly in two streams again. Before the streams disappeared he inhaled them back into firm dedicated nostrils, designed genetically for copious quantities of oxygen inhalation needed to support such a muscular taught body frame.

The cigar holding hand went limp at the wrist causing a dark gray ash ring to plop upon the pedestrian table top and blanket out like tiny dust particles.

The old man asked a test question, as he put it, then ejected the question.

"What's big tech?"

"I don't know. What's big tech?" I answered.

"A little weenie searching for relevance."

"What relevance?"

"Not what, but who. Miss Relevance. Disappeared a little while back, to places unknown, for now."

"Did I pass the test?"

The old man nodded in between thick-smoked cigar puffs. I wondered what next, again. The puffs of smoke betrayed an aromatic hint of burnt animal skin. A window to my left permitted a shimmer of the day's gray tone. A curtain which framed the window jiggled a bit. I wondered why. No air or wind I felt. No heard echoes against the interior room walls or from objects on the cabinet shelves of the connected open kitchen area.

"Okay, what is it?" the old man creature asked.

"Just wondering what's going on here, in this place. Don't know its name. You know, where we are."

The old man wore loosely a short sleeved white tee shirt. Looked like he had been wearing it for a while based on the worn and stretched appearance of cloth in the biceps and neck areas. The right sleeve end twitched a bit, as if something brushed against it, but again, no object became visible. I could feel the movement of air as if something passed by invisible.

"Oh geesh," I thought. The old man noticed my face expression of concern.

"No worries. Just some friends," the old man said.

"Friends?" My face revealed thoughts to him.

"Sure. They took me in, allowed me to enter, to play with."

I didn't initially know how to interpret such a statement.

Either as warning, or as rationalization for rogue winds piercing the walls of a dying house. Then it occurred to me. Spirits may inhabit and share the residence spaces. The comforting temperature of a cooled draft seemed to call to me. Prickled my skin.

The old man stood up, bumping the wooden chair backwards but not enough in distance for him to straighten his spine. The chair accommodated such a creature miscalculation. It moved away from the old man's legs, permitting more room for him to straighten the body.

"As long as they're not agitated, alarmed, as it were, we're fine," the old man advised. "Come on, I'll show you around."

When he stood fully, his height seemed to vary, as if he bounced a bit. The spine seemed to extend his body hire. No evidence of skin tightness revealed itself.

I was confused. How is that happening in the old man's body. I wondered. Looked up at the ceiling, then heard a sound, like tiny gears moving, looked down, and noticed the sweat pants old man creature wore seemed too long in the leg length, but in seconds stretched upwards until they perfectly fit his lower body structure, almost like the old man's legs elevated to fit the space around them, as necessary. I wondered if old man creature's arms could extend in the same manner.

The look of the place spoke uneventful, but the creature and his invisible and inanimate friends betrayed otherwise. Still, no hostile intent or action had been presented. I followed behind the old man creature. A kitchen cabinet creaked open only inches. Something inside there moved, or exited. I felt a tug on my pants cuff, looked down, nothing seen there.

Old man creature's foot dragged a bit weighty soon enough, but still able to scrape along the yellowed faux tiled floor. This old guy seemed happy, as if he didn't know better. He had claimed happiness as his own right of existence.

"Have you been around long, I mean here?" old man asked.

"No, not really. Sort of woke up one day, and I found myself out there," as I pointed towards the gray outside area.

"You're lucky they didn't corner you in a tractor beam and force field fencing. Can't see it, but sure can feel the squeeze of it when activated," old man creature advised in a low guttural groan.

"How did you know it was there?" I had to ask.

"I came over here from another town, after the soldiers and residents ended up in a turf war, trashing the town in the process," the old creature said, then continued, "I could sense the beam, humming sounds of it. Walked around the boundary for a good while, until I found my way here. The spirits here guided me. Couldn't see them, but they moved around, disturbed the ground sand farther out, then the grassy areas around here. I follow their sounds and movements."

"You weren't worried they might attack you?"

"Sure, but they seemed to push in the direction to here."

"They didn't hurt you."

"No, just seemed to tease me a bit. Seems to be in their nature. A bit of taunts and spooks about, but nothing violent. At least not this time. Another time when I went exploring near there, a patrol of soldiers came by and the invisible spirits turned into banshees, knocked over some of the soldiers. They scattered and eventually left while calling reinforcements somewhere out there that never came."

This found place of my current uncertain in time tenancy offered an opportunity to learn about the Brim life. Satisfy tastes and desires according to government protocol, and all existence may remain calm. Lust for life is an exaltation. If the feeling leads to love, it is expressed by a spark in the mind, released as inspiration, similar to energies of exploding stars and supernova moments.

There existed many times a difference between what we remembered and what really happened. Ants are social creatures. So are humans. Each awaits death which may occur at any time moment. Sometimes the best way to do nothing is to do something. The opposite is also true. The journey of life maybe a long one, along a rugged path, but the feral step into the land of death, just one step, and there the journey becomes much longer. To be, or not.

That's a cool place. Wonder if they've got any bugs there. Three types of creatures existent on this planet. The thought echoed in great aunt Helen's voice. She spoke in a high pitch of sound, but her words rolled smoothly as a hot summer's brook. All other living things are viruses of one type or another, basically cannibals of meat or vegetation sources. All attempted survival in a great war unintended but necessary.

The sentient beings subjected to continued survival status were classified as human, humanoid, and hybrid-creature. Much lesser beings in some areas identified as inanimate animates, spirits trapped between life and after-life, and life forms previously classified as fairy tale characters which spring into existence amidst this world either as by the seeds of mind powers, or the experimentations of wild-eyed overlords in the ruling government. Examples are trovants and portal tombs and dolmens.

Trovants are rock-like creatures. They can move along the ground somewhat like snails but much faster if necessary. They can transform their surface structure and texture from a solid rock feel to a jelly type of substance flexibility. Rumored to be good hunters and protectors. Portal tombs and dolmen are located on burial grounds, serving as structures able to transport the dead into an afterlife. Wind and Shadow Souldiers likely transported their existence capabilities in such a manner. Rumor, myth, reality served many masters.

The overlords, overseers, and converted minions swore allegiance to the one party allowed to govern. Official opposition groups had been quickly crushed, extinguished long ago. We called those missing people and creatures the disappeared, but they remained remembered. I tried to seek my place in this morbid flesh mix.

Healer beamed as a choice. Wherever I visited, whoever I encountered seemed to benefit from my attention to the needs of place, person, and creature. At first my presence made wary the residents as the sudden appearance of a stranger inadvertently but understandably brewed cause. My presence may have raised safety concerns. Residents of all species likely wondered if another government soldier came by only to recon and spy. Fairies and sprites didn't seem to mind the visitor. Just another target for their mischief and cantankerous nature to prod and probe.

Such reactions gave me pause. Had overseer minions altered my mind? I judged the intrusions to my body would eventually give up the ghost of such actions in dream states of repose. I began to realize reprogramming entered the equation of change I came to achieve, although slowly, in body and mind quirks unfamiliar. I deduced such given the surgical markings applied to my varied skin areas of joints and internal organ locations.

Those in power controlled the truth. Steal it from the weak as a means to test it and reproduce it or retool it for their own totalitarian purposes. Dole it out later at their convenient leisure, or pound it out with weapons furnished to their loyal minion regulars.

Survivors bore some choice in the existence formula. Some acquiesced to reformulation governed by needs and desires of varying degrees. Those degrees generally fell into a few select categories such as food, shelter, and family commiserations.

Viruses unknown spread rampant, unleashed by vigorous war weapons fallout, and some viruses seemed spread by distinct, intentional programmed processes intended to survive and mutate amidst the remaining living inhabitants of any species form. The whole of the Brim lands seemed to be laid out as an experimental world. Inhabitants couldn't quite master a mentality grasp on what species entity higher in intelligence and technology strength rolled out such a plan. The only certainty concerned the view of a takeover by an ever-present, preternatural warring race previously unidentified in the solar system of the Brim planetoid.

Old man creature invited me outside to the low-level wooden porch just at the end of the door stoop. The dark gray night shroud had fallen upon the land but a black darkness refused a call, as it had for more than a few generations of existence. We each sat in lawn chairs, as he called them. First he pulled them out from under the porch, then opened them like a hinged door, laid them on metal stemmed legs. I noticed the position of the chairs, upon seating ourselves in them, allowed a distant view of crystalline light dots massed close together beyond the tips of the oak forest terrain. What looked like night stars were city lights. The tree shadows crafted an appearance of an overly large ice cream cone. My questions started.

"Why don't we go there, to that city?"

"That's not a city. Not now," he responded.

The cigar aroma smelled sweeter in this air of low and calm light. A brief rustling sound below the porch floor ticked loud alarms in my head. The old man said to ignore them, the sprites. The cigar smell makes them a bit high and dopey in physical fits.

"So, what is it?" I continued the quest for answers.

He took a short huff of the cigar sweetness, then spoke during exhale, scattered the smoke to the delight of the loopy sprites under the porch.

"A death trap."

"How so?"

"It's a one-way trip. Those who enter never exit."

My imagination didn't know whether to spark or fizzle at the thought. I chose to energize the spark further.

"Surely there are some living creatures there."

"Maybe. Not really. Creatures, but not living as you remember a life's day."

I measured his response as odd, given he didn't know my past any better than I could recall it.

"Soldiers, maybe," I answered as first response, given my experience in what I believed was a small city or town during reprogramming.

"You could call them that," he responded, retracting a short, bellowed puff for a second bite of the taste.

"Humanoid?" I had to ask. Why not. Time laid out no constraints in this place thus far.

"Not in the least," he responded, less patient in tone. The remainder of the cigar appeared like a tree stump, short of standing, but not yet gone.

"Yes, it does." I accommodated his previous motions of a need for measured silence into contemplation time. I had to imagine the conversation parry as follows until the entrance of a needed mind void.

"What does it mean?

"That far away light connects to the light we sometimes see across the road. The light across the road traps your anatomy, dissolves it, then transports it to the city light."

"Oh."

"There you materialize in anatomy restored, but the transmission process creates a chromosome loss, likely filed and stored for government testing purposes."

"Ouch."

"Yes. Ouch. You're not who you were anymore. You become whatever they need in forms of labor, shelter, or food."

"Food?"

"Yes. Food. Do you really need me to elaborate?"

"Shelter?"

"Yes, for micro-organisms storage until a status of ready for use materializes."

"Labor?"

"For any purpose of use connected to need at the moment. A walking, talking if allowed by questions asked, storage warehouse."

"That isn't life."

"It is, for their benefit. Only for their benefit."

Old man creature grunted. The cigar had sizzled out on a destination to no use status. I looked over at him. A bot of a snort and snore sound oozed from his long and wide nostrils which had hibernated below long fur threads.

"She's almost ready for birth time."

The voice sound startled me. Not sure where it originated from. Maybe the long and somewhat bushy patches of hair ringed around his lips down to the jaw cavern masked flesh motions. I looked around after a taught body tense generated by the previous vision moments. His words portrayed not useful meaning to my mind. I began to realize this place wasn't exactly what it seemed. Many veils of understanding have yet to be lifted for me.

A sprite made an appearance tipsy but near quiet in action. It looked at me from the porch edge, with my own eyes peering back at me as mirror image.

"Nice trick. Nice, even in loopy status. A cunning strange." One day we'll find out, too late, the science fictions authors were always right.

A Nest Half Full

Sleep called. Ruminations begged for a simple rest. Thirsts unquenched yet again. In the subconscious world's surrender, a fight still raged. Awaken. Continue. The battle's not lost. The mind net remained to subjugate sentience efforts. In the Brim's somnambulant shadows, an ever-present conflagration of battles continued. Battles of creatures and viruses and many non-human beings, faster of motions, weaponized of strong jaw bit clamps applied, winged stings, claws sharp, nails hewn into razors whether of land or sea birth. Humans survived by learning when to flee, when to fight.

All creatures suffered the same rules. Many unknown viruses had attacked the body systems. Immunities developed randomly and slowly. Severe sickness during recovery times doomed many village populations of human, humanoid, and hybrid creatures alike. All other biological systems including plant, animal, and insect life suffered a similar trial and error process. A callous nature fit for an amoral societal structure prevailed, evolved. The art of stealth became a crucial survival mechanism in all societies whether flora or fauna.

Creatures generally attacked external organs of each other. Wolves, snakes, wasps, animals human, humanoid, or hybrid. No exceptions. The bipedal also developed poisons from berries and wild flowers, set traps with them amidst known lesser creature's feeding grounds, to avoid close hazardous contact conditions during assaults. Spit, sweat, excrement became weapons when they were none to remain infected with the known viruses. Fear served as motivator and mediator for all types of life. Injury, death hovered in the shadows ready to spring.

Viruses didn't suffer the fear curse. No forethought wasted attack time. No preparations carefully plotted. Viruses ate, anything encountered, by any means necessary or available in matters of atmosphere or object or animal contact. Even death didn't serve as permanent extinction. It merely served as a limbo of rest, restitution, evolution in phases when turnaround time evolved quickly and quicker than many of the remaining extant life forms. The least sentient of life forms evolved into murder armies outnumbering all living things. The ruling overlords fought these invisible warriors also.

Viruses also attacked other viruses. A near undefeatable whole of entities could evolve unstoppable. For all living animal creatures some type of uncontaminated food source was crucial for continued existence. In a specific manner, viruses acted like humans, humanoids, and hybrids. If no other food sources were available, attacks against their own allies and kin would serve their moral structure for survival. Cycles endless. Endless cycles. From a non-virus perspective, it all seemed repetitions of motions pointless. If eternity exists, it exists in the land of the virus. Humans and similar life forms believe, generally, in a future path of existence eternal. Otherwise, what is the purpose of life at all? Such a question doesn't exist or require deep contemplation for the virus world. Eternity is their singular domain.

From a perspective of more sentient life forms, such a world existed as a sick game of cat and mouse, life and death match, conjoined worlds of horror happiness. The sickest reality of it all remained. In order for one organism to exist it must drain life from another organism. No exceptions. Food stood needed for survival in the biological entity of life form service. In all the existence formulas a sea of death flowed along and around as the trap waiting to be sprung.

He awoke, still in battered, patched, hybrid form. "I feel like shit," he told himself, or at least, his body said so. Brief contemplations sprung upon him out of dream state, poked at his mind. "What a furking sadistic mess. Who or what produced this idea of existence?" At least final death remained a few steps behind, winded during the chase.

Here's a strange ambush. Viruses and four-legged creatures of land, and two or more legged critters of the skies of avian or insect life, and two-legged hominids shared one planet we refer to as the nature. Nature, the least sentient of all, rules the ground and sea. All living things shared inhabitance at their peril. The only living entity among all sentient and non-sentient life forms, humans, contemplate about the who what when where why and how of it all. I've stumbled upon a kind of life philosophy. Sounds stoic. Is there a difference between to be and not to be? That proposition is the question? If there is no difference, the question is pointless, which leads to an existence not of purpose, except to please the mind and body entity until expiration time. Perhaps we humans learn from each other for a purpose, but the best reward possible is not in the hoped-for afterlife. The purpose is to promote and achieve a harmonious current life. Creative nonhumans seems to have by and large accomplished this task purpose. Harmony, unless the hunger plague strikes and then pre-learned and inbred instinctual survival skills kick in.

Ultimate death isn't a long-term worry for the less sentient creatures. They are only concerned about where they are going in the present time. We humans think about concerns of where is the destination after this life, too. Our instinct for survival has been blunted, stunted by worry of a life circumstance after the one provided to us now, here.

Humans are obsessed with the prospect of ultimate death. I ruminated about similar issues often. Something in my brain locked out the answers almost as if the lock mechanism were inserted prior to my birth. I've thought so since an early age. While reading, writing, studying always looking for the answer., I get close, then it runs away, floats, speeds into shadows. I know an answer exists, is there, out there somewhere, or locked away in my brain recesses somewhere, but I can't find the key to that place. I've seen other humans die, dying. Friends, relatives, random encounters with citizens who died minutes ago lying in the middle of a street as if acting dead in an opera scene. In the faces of the dead, I saw a point of purpose lost. I could see an answer prodding at them, almost crawling out of the forehead, then an expression of some revelation beamed, but their words uttered unintelligible to me, similar to my time at Aunt Helen's deathbed side.

Maybe a wicked trick of near expiration moments. The eventual answer, the show finale, was only revealed at the end of life's theater production, but the seconds leading to final communication have gone away and no longer a vowel of sound possible.

Maybe the dying remember something they wanted to say or tell but forgot or couldn't be told due to how the revelation in words might sound. Too embarrassing or frightful, or maybe a piece of wisdom they had long ago discovered but tossed aside remains not relevant or important, but in last life moments consider the thought most important. At my age, don't pee on your slippers seems as good advice as any. Slapped myself. Come on. Not yet too old for this broken-down place of a planetoid.

The Quaint Parry

"There will always be more than once a man who expresses love actually loves, or feigns to love for selfish and self-serving fashion or form, until the day you die." He continued.

"And there will always be those men who appreciated how you made love to them. Those memories haunted them, for a long, long time, recalled more significantly in night time masturbation moments. At climax, unnatural howls emanated into outside ears close to the open summer window."

She sipped from the wine glass. The red liquid pleased her palette. Seemed pleased in the thoughts espoused by his words. A religious zeal came to her mind, then her "right" response sounded a tone of sarcasm. Her opinion continued.

"Any more wisdoms you'd like to rush off your chest?" Her prelude to a second wine sip cornered lips perks close to the glass edge After the sip moments sparked further perky words.

"Maybe. Maybe, baby."

Seminal thoughts begged for his attention. "Nice hair. Delectable smell." Wondered how a touch would feel.

The parry ended, short and sour. The honor of lovers always remained a test of wills. Every day, something good, something gone. As humanity's curse weaved cunning quirks among the populace. The quirks of moment and chance, and opportunity lost in the flights of sparrow flocks low in the sky yet tall in mind. Daylight sounds danced to such human tunes and lives. Coffee or tea. Bread or bagel. Butter or jam. Fork or spoon. Wait for hurry. Facial expressions kind or sour. Choices captured upon the hour.

The Tedium band played loud and long, casually interrupted by the chaos cymbals, or sometimes the gong. Church bell rings. Bee buzzes. Laughs, cackles, and many other day bourn senses clash.

A buckle of the knees reminds him to properly calibrate his next moments modified by age, or nagging injury old, or ground surface foot hazards invented like pavement curbs, or fallen from the sky tree branches or bird skat, or careless objects deemed trash disposed like rejected second dates. Unplanned annoyances of sound like phone rings, car horns, corner barkers hocking wares or free offers printed upon papers or balloons. "Step right up. It'll brighten your day!" Price to be determined. Time spent is a price paid. Unredeemable. Happiness isn't guaranteed. Extended warranty, for a single second. How a voice dances with words opens a window to the mind.

We play at being wise and noble, but still, nature has a way of parry. All choices seek a destiny. There's more to the equation, but little time to process.

Mistakes

One of the most beautiful incendiary delights of the new Brim involved efforts to establish a bond of trust amongst the population at large. Initially, the efforts drew many supporters. The more skeptical of citizens stayed back, in the shadows as means to watch as test the implications of such societal efforts. Some prospective views began to reveal the new truths of such a planetoid indoctrination. Parts of the populace failing to reveal a cheerful outlook were treated as second-class citizens. Resources became limited in their community areas. Requests for government run maintenance services fell off the jurisdictional map as if the communities no longer existed in the grand scheme of service and need. The attention they needed, they paid for in taxes and licensing fees withered and died. Daily functionality proved impossible. Electricity, the water purification services, a security deprivation invited those of ill intentions to take over and control daily life. Such lifestyle devolutions seemed programmed to proceed until the localities were no longer sustainable.

Great movements of the populace resulted in the ring of death bells for many communities which concluded into a ghost town existence suitable for criminals, vagrants, chemically diseased and biologically diseased. Such living conditions became deemed as death camps; the places where the cycles of life shortened dramatically. Those people who failed to jump on the new Brim government wagon were silently deemed non-compatible. Choked off from resources needed for livable conditions. Eventually, hunted down by minions of the government overseers. Under government beckons for efficiency enlightenment, a permitted by decree elimination exploited by varied means plagued the new Brim. Disappearance, removal to re-education centers similar to the decrepit and dying areas bearing uncivil and diseased citizens, or warrants issued for capture by any means necessary resulted. The warrant holder was government remunerated as means to encourage captures or exchange of information leading to a capture. Public shaming of those individuals caught usually resulted as a warning to citizens, and as means to scare family and friends into considering compliance with the overseer's demands for efficiency.

Initially, government announcements of a new Brim and how to keep it efficient seemed a benign request, but eventually the request became more direct until it evolved into demands, and finally into commands. The command effect became a virus unto itself, infecting the minds and thinking and reactions across all lands. Skeptics and mockers of such developments provided public speeches, the most famous of which stated, "They can take all they want except this blade of grass!" Not long after such an incantation, even blades of grass disappeared in the more populated Brim areas. The government had won out. Only the body count remained for calculation.

Chaos reigned. Chaos ruled. Chaos loved. Chaos fed. Chaos bred. Dangerous dead. The place where socially calculated numbers determined existence levels and form. Number of humans. Number of humanoids. Number of hybrid creatures. For some reason, the number of overseers and minions were not included in the calculations, which skewed the final results, prejudicially.

The cities were rumored to be locked down upon initial implementation of the new Brim societal norms. The living conditions fumigated by disappearances. Other rumors revealed a totalitarian societal structure where usable citizens worked as slaves for the overlords. Their needs are deemed essential to an efficient working of the population system.

If the rumors could be any worse, another spread about reconditioning methods instituted for the body, mind, and soul of those deemed unworthy. Once converted into a worth status, a future society purpose remained uncertain. Prophets, prognosticators, propagandists, provocateurs, government agents designed to monitor enforcement of daily proclamations circled in the rumor mills.

A post script of rumor still existed, but didn't gain much traction because discussing it instilled fears of persecution and disappearance. The elites of overlord culture reserved some reconditioning centers for their private use, it was said. The rumor developed from that situational status into the possibility of a mistake during reconditioning of the god-like figure, Daed Suoregnad. The reconditioning failed but not before significant brain function capability had been scrambled. Suoregnad remained alive, but unaware of any sentience of his true self. A slave rebellion also had been in force for some time in the same location. The hordes descended upon the facility, unaware of the occupants, then destroyed it and every living thing inside.

It had been shut down, never to be reported about publicly. Perhaps some of the persecutions and disappearances were fueled by a search for Suoregnad. Attempts to eat from the plate of memories gave no clue to quality or flavor. The taste was bland.

The Gods' Conundrum

According to great Aunt Helen, even gods ruled gods. A hierarchical structure existed, mimicked by humans, humanoids, and creatures in many planetary cultures. I pictured a god still having needs. If a god suddenly found themselves seated on a second-floor bathroom toilet seat lid, bent over with some slight back pain as result, reached forward and struggled to get the fingers-grasped toenail clippers properly edged across the large toenail of the left foot, please realize such actions prescient in the mind means the world, as they've known it, has just ended, as such an effort would seem so foreign to a supernatural mindset as it could be thought of as a next life's moment. The next moments were subject to a much different than expected progression. Perhaps cursed as punishment of expulsion from the god realm for a prohibited indiscretion. Relegation to a planetoid realm would mean a loss of some if not all supernatural power, but not necessarily the usual powers of lesser god's. Don't fret, the god would think. They allowed me some time to acclimate.

It was pridefully bold of my mind to imply the current status of my essence as derived of a lesser god's punishment, to be interred at the Brim planetoid for a time period uncertain. Imagination can spark from thought fires like sudden tinder spouts upward, exuding crackles, dispersing tiny flame shards into ash after short airward travels. Orgasmic moments of nature's mix and maw.

Nature, whether triggered by human or animal instinct, eventually evokes moments of wild supremacy imposed upon all living and object things around it. Momentary growls and shouts of "I'm still here!" as effort to prove relevance continues unabated. A fear bursts sensibility, perhaps. Such living entities are not gods in any conventional sense. Maybe squirrels see the larger creatures as gods, yet the tiny creature still, in agitated moments, attempts a nip of the hands reaching towards it instigated by fears of the unknown. A petting maneuver to show friendly intentions, or a jab to ensnare a little creature viewed only as a food source. Intentions generally hidden amongst all creatures, especially upon first contact. Friend or foe. Encroacher or protector. Harmony is earned, never presumed, in this world. From time-to-time harmony is destroyed by distrust, or by a misreading of intentions. Time and experience tells whether intentions are noble, or acts performed as deceit spreads.

My dream time impatiently nagged restless thoughts. After all of the creeping around and hiding at old man creatures place, and my nagging feelings of being perceived as an unknown entity that had mysteriously entered, I tried to ascertain whether distractions and deceits of sounds, of knocks, creaks, bangs, tipping of knickknacks and objects in the living room, dining area and kitchen, I discovered the creatures vision, eyes, facial features and eventually more of the physic reminded me of a female accent. Maybe she had the biological ability to disguise herself as such a gender during times of stress. It had been the first time we each met. Her scent seemed to have changed, too. A bit musky, but ending in a sweetish aroma at the tail end of breath exhales. I became intrigued to learn more about the biology of her, and curious to explore her true intentions for allowing me into her structure inhabitance space.

Maybe I had dazed in and out of dream state during our first encounter because I suddenly felt safe in her presence. I didn't know her moral capacities or true intentions just yet. She could have murdered me in my sleep. My newfound senses created previously in the government lab experimentations had yet to become fully known to me.

The revelations streamed somewhat helpful and timely. A new instinct defensive mechanism had either been placed or activated in me, of which I previously was unaware. Gene therapy had evolved as the rage of elite societal groups many years earlier, and prior to the war induced apocalypse. The cycle of infinite gray outdoors, blanketed by permanent cloud cover, impacted the remaining creatures, activated new survival skills development as means to co-exist amidst the new nature system all around the Brim.

Food deliveries still arrived at this place, so it had apparently been added to the governments map of useful humans, humanoids, hybrids still considered exploitable for government dominion and service. I had a while back deduced the overlords had ceased a pursuit of me since I was now likely considered untraceable. I trusted my senses would have been able to detect a tracking system biological or electronic.

Whether advanced versions of me could accomplish the government's capture mission I wasn't sure. They never stopped experimentation or enhancement efforts of those yet to be discarded in the disappearance category. If I had been declared not useful, my mind would no longer be able to chronicle these adventures in memories. Could be I was still deemed as a Test Case.

I often suffered from near paralyzing paranoia episodes, especially amidst environs unfamiliar. Spirits tended to scare me at a younger age. Spoke to me, or at least audible in my mind. A genetic trait attributable to my ethnic heritage and specifically, family blessing or curse. Despite how common was their presence in the places I encountered from an early age under the auspices of Aunt Helen's influence, the issue of judging their true intentions, whether mischief or knowledge tidbits, remained a sticky wicket.

After undergoing the government experimentations performed on my body I wondered if my genetic system could instinctively mask a true clinical assessment of my origin and potential capability, much like an athlete or avid book knowledge studier tested physical and mental abilities and limits while traversing the aging course. A more humored take sounded like the operating room of my brief internment. "Now, what do we have here? Useful or not?" The laser pen applied to the disabled body bedded, strapped upon a thin layer of cold metal would determine a fate, piece by bittered piece. Face up, face down, or sideways, usefulness avenues to be determined.

Sounds my gracious host made outside while jiggling the lock on the food box whetted my appetite for the contents. I heard her voice raised almost like in a curse tone as her large hands and long finger tips coaxed the box lock to free the lid of the container. Removal of the contents completed; she stalked a path back into the residence. Her footsteps sank hard into the flooring, creaked rigid echoes into the staircase which led to the second floor. I slid out from under the bed cover, sat up, and awaited a meal my hunger urges ached for an arrival.

"Apologies," she offered. "The deliveries have been erratic in frequency lately."

A loud stirring of tree limbs and brush in the distance outside revealed a scuffle underway for a neighbor's food box sources. Who or what competed for the food uncertain. A new predator in the neighborhood, government people checking on whether the assigned person or family attempted the food collection as assigned, or a trap had been laid to capture someone in need of disappearance.

Another Day

The following day passed by slowly and predictable. Today did not. Time is not kind. Chasing memories attracts hungry flies into the mind trap. My perspective now ignited into third person as cautions against government capture or other prey stalkers. He had slept in after and missed the last meal time. Awoke in the evening hours, which meant the outside light had turned a darker shade of gray. His body he determined, after phasing from dream state to awake time, revealed the surface below him was outside ground in the nearby woods. He could still sense the house location where he had slept but only as a distant aroma. The impression of the ground surface didn't seem familiar. The surface revealed a stone and dirt surface much like an old and infrequently used walking path. A stir nearby caused him to crawl quickly toward brush cover to hide. The wind kicked up a bit to reveal a scent familiar. His new friend from the house searched him out to provide some food.

Each of them genetically are of creature blood. She is pure blood of her species. He is a mutt of human, humanoid, and hybrid. He marveled at her serene calmness in this outside area under the oaks and ash trees. She seemed more at home here than in the house.

Needed some introspection view to analyze the moment. Please pardon the mindset switches. They sting me too. I still retained enough human gene sensitivities to become bothered by the stage of moment. My patches of hair stood on end, tightened the fit of an already too tight shirt, but displayed pockmarks through the shredded part of these long pants. Repurposed my perspective.

They shared mutual memories and a dim recall for a reason. If they could reliably trust these memories, each would discover a similar history collection. One aspect of similarity concerned age assessments. She believed her existence age spanned 60 or more Brim years; the counting confounded somewhat by the gray Brim days difficult to check off. To him, she looked in her thirty's. He revealed a similar age to hers, but admitted he felt much older, and some days the air breathed into him a much younger age feeling.

"Something's on your mind," she said.

"What makes you say that?" He wondered where such a thought in her mind originated.

"When you sleep, you talk," she said, " whispers only, but my ears still hear."

"What do I say?"

"Seems you repeat worlds of the person talking to you, mostly," she said.

"My aunt talks to me. At least, I remember her words, from the past."

"What if she is talking with you," she said.

"I've thought of that," he said.

"My mate did the same thing. Talked with me during sleep. Mostly pleasant, but sometimes in a warning tone."

"Did the warnings pan out?" he asked.

"Yes," is all she said.

He had to ask. "Where's your mate now?"

She looked over at the tractor beam area, then pointed, and said, "Somewhere out there."

He wondered why her mate had left her. She gave an answer as if she read my mind. I've heard of such talents. Aunt Helen displayed a similar trait, or maybe she was wise enough to read thoughts based on the mannerisms of the listener.

"I'm sure he's okay," he said, trying to help arrest any emotional high tide the conversation may have blown in.

"He is, now. Some rough times. I've lost his connection, of spirit."

I didn't know what to say, if anything, in response. I let her words float around in my head a bit. Psychic ability?

Premonition strength? Paranoia? Normal worries of a loved one concerned of their mate's travels and itinerary?

Maybe her mate searched for food and never returned. Not an uncommon event.

"He'll be back," she said in a certainty of tone.

He understood her reason for concern. To lose a friend, lover, began to offer the soul hunger pangs emotional. Then she addressed him, smirking a bit, in the way a depressed person does so.

"You've met him, in a way."

He wanted to ask in what way, but his mind took over the question. It raced through the facts of the first physical encounter in her house. A male with a cigar in hand, seated at the dining room table, asking riddle questions. Stalking the nature and purpose of my visit. Understandable in such new Brim encounters.

"I was the male seated at the table, emulating him in appearance and mannerisms, while I assessed any potential threats or harm engendered during your entrance upon this tiny space in the woods."

She had pretended to be the male she knew, her mate. She possessed transmutation qualities. The overloads would love to study her, he guessed.

More noises they heard in the woods, from a bit of ways off in distance. His instinct said hide. Hers remained calm. "Why do we hide?" she asked. "To survive," he responded. "No. No I mean why hide, us?" she asked. "Not sure," he said, "seems the right thing to do." Some measured silence of conversation ruled the time passing until the distance noises audibly faded. Each had realized from experience that their scents were not readily recognizable to predators who had never encountered them. She offered some advice.

"I sense your concerns. Trust me, for every heavenly moment, there are ten sent directly from hell."

"An accumulation of moments still escapes me," he said. He also thought it bold of her to expect his trust on such short notice. They hadn't shared enough time together to explore an acquaintance of any measure.

As creature breeds, each of them seemed rare in the predator recognition histories. He suggested, now that his prey hackles had been ignited, he be allowed to prowl around the house interior to learn more about its history and purpose in this woodland region. She readily agreed, succeeded by a long, warm yawn.

During her yawn he spied a slight vertical breach in her facial skin between her right ear and nose as if the skin had been overstretched. It popped into his view as odd, but he discarded the thought almost immediately. In doing so, his eyes glanced at her hair. The center hairline starting at the forehead seemed a bit off center whereas before it revealed a more symmetrical appearance. To accompany the yawn, she stretched out her arms at the sides and revealed long and thick hair strands and bands comparable to an Ursus Arctos or brown bear.

He wondered about the extent of body coverage upon her skin areas. A quick glance at her lower leg and feet areas revealed no shoes, but a similar type of hairy skin covering which extended upward to the rim of her long and wrinkled dress line. He extended his arm towards her to assist an upright and two footed standing effort, but she lurched forward on all fours, then pushed herself upward at the spot where her hands pressed upon the ground. They proceeded in an upright walk to her residence.

Inside the house, his urgent need for exploration had somewhat waned in energy but not of spirit. He searched out targets of revelation in drawers and cabinets. The doors of each intrigued him of mysteries magical. She moved over to the living room reclining chair in a darker lit corner space to steal a nap. He noticed her rest seeking demeanor, so his instincts entered predator stealth mode. Something's coming. He could feel it. Annihilation.

He tried to keep his mind focused on the sundries search within the drawers, but random wanders along the avenue of youthful memories, when he was a whole person and not displaced parts of many being persisted. The complications of those times seemed simple compared to these recent times, when the tiniest moments of assumed prosperity became stomped by the dominion of overlords. Going up the ladder to the roof, where we could see ever much better, risked exposure to government eyes.

He continued the drawers search. Inside one he found many photographs torn in half. Perhaps an emotional moment had sparked such finality. Many letters penned on frayed yellow paper expressed the imminent doom feelings scattered amongst previous residents. Earrings but none matched as pairs. Perhaps the fashion of the time, or more likely confirmation of a lack of opportunity to replace trinkets seemed no longer an entertainment. Pliers, cut wires, rusted hand tools no longer usable.

Broken dreams, twisted minds, fleeing souls ruled these days cruelly. A story authored by sordid entities bent on control. This place seemed held together by duct tape and string, and the residents were all out of string. Not sure what the previous owner was thinking. Maybe lost a loved one or family member. Maybe a visitor wandering wild, looking for any substance, chemical, injected to rid the mind of inflicted horrors. The situation wasn't much different in the details, regardless. The overloads scouted this place previously, perhaps became aware of mischief which made them worry, decided to stamp it out. The residents I had failed to present themselves as a threat even minimal in potential impact. The government feared this place. Not many children are born here for them to steal and program. No miscreants to reform.

These overseers looked to find resources. And not as before when fields full of sheep meandered, ate, and grew their wool fluffy and neat. The seeds of our overlord master's plans were everywhere, in every being and creature and food box delivery. Their tasks grew heavier, long, and deep. We put as many rocks in their satchels as feasible. Made their efforts grueling and tiresome. Memories heavy they accrued at our expense. Memories of distraction. Memories of shame. Memories of weakness. Memories of blame. But memories of comfort? Those memories fled out the back door, left open, by us. Sometimes a memento hidden is better off unfound.

An Uninvited Guest

Commotion sounds broke the air outside loud. Truth strikes loud as a hurricane wind in this part of the Brim.

Such devastation is only allowed from lips of the overseers, minions of the government, rustlers of residents deemed gone bad. After they left, explosions and vocal screams echoed from a distance. The remainders of use, their captured or worse fated supplicants viewed such episodes as rules enforcements.

I walked over to the kitchen to see what foods may still lurk in the refrigerator, relieved this house had been spared hands of chaos. Before my hand touched the handle I noticed a motion in the small mirror stuck on the door. My right nose nostril itched a bit, then a fright overtook me. An unexpected guest appeared near the front door. Somehow the door had opened and closed behind the guest without my ears picking up the motion sounds of the hinges and the click of the latch. I further became freaked inside, worried why my creature senses didn't alert me to her presence outside before she entered. I say she, because the which accompanied her presence exuded a scent familiar of such gender. I sniffed again and was not dissuaded from my first impression. I still didn't turn around. Didn't want to provide any threatening movements in her direction. I wondered whether the house host had stepped out, or whether she remained in a deep rest, unaware of these proceedings.

The guest didn't move, just looked around. Feigned as if she didn't notice me, or smell my scent yet. Maybe she was dazed by the outdoor commotion earlier, a part of it, escaped it, and now in the cool down biological period of licking away emotional wounds. I concentrated on her eyes. Glazed a bit, they appeared. No physical disruption from inflicted body wounds apparent from the small mirror's perspective. She then licked her lips as if thirsty, or maybe hungry.

I hadn't opened the refrigerator yet, wondered what she savored during her taste contemplations. The it hit me. I shuddered. Me. She fancied me. I didn't want to know in what capacity special. Tortured by such thoughts I became. Wondered if she had imposed them upon me through some mind trick. My paranoid instincts ignited.

Her lips touch my neck. Soft lips for a person or creature who had completed the trek from the nearest village and not chapped or chafed at her mouth area. Wondered if she had snuck up on me while my thoughts clouded the mirror's reflection. Was her stealth so cunning that she could sneak up from behind and come so close? If she had previously been captured and programmed as a government minion I could imagine such a strategy used to soften the instinct ability of her prey to judge reality. During such worry, she began another assault upon my right cheek, starting at the lower jaw ridge. Lips and flexible tongue worked a magic soothing. My thoughts freaked out, but a physical stimulation pleasant had set the trap.

I again lost focus on her for a bit, not the mirror's fault. Mine. My focus had become dampened, distracted by bizarre thoughts of danger dancing with delight.

I refocused on the mirror. She halted her tongue to jaw to cheek movements by her eyes seemed to measure a part of my neck for some still mysterious purpose. Whatever her saliva had done to my conscious self, it seemed mystical in nature. Calmed me so much as if I had forgotten calm as a lost feeling.

The heat in her breath streamed unfamiliar to me. She let her long, light silky hair flow along the side of my face. Each pore of my skin oozed a passion disabling. The mirror refused to reveal an accurate picture of her face. Sometimes it appeared, sometimes it melted away her features from my eyesight.

My entire world seemed to end when any part of her touches left me, as if she baited my attention stronger to hook and capture an emotional response. Such responses drain energy. Mine. She was stealing my energy. The energy remaining in me I focused on the parts of her I could see of her face, hair, neck. All blurs to me now. She seemed to just want to use me up. Abuse me.

In my younger days I always worried about what might be behind me. I felt touches there, but upon checking a nearby mirror, or turning around, only a few times realized a physical presence. A schoolchild pranker, or a casual errant bump in a crowd. An inability to completely see created a fear. I fought efforts of comfort. Feared my rear guard would become complacent, errant.

I practiced ways to defeat the fear. Never sat with my back facing an open space if I could help it. Sat close to a wall, the wall at or up against my back. Sat in the farthest bench from the church alter, because then there remained only one wall I couldn't ascertain for potential danger. Never liked the mystery of the back pat administered by someone behind me, even if it was intended as a friendly hello gesture. Sometimes the gesture struck like a threatening blow requiring a tensing of muscle to restrain a push or shove type of strike. What lay in the dark. A spider, a rock, an approaching hand. These possibilities tortured my mind, or at least, the damages potential of such contacts.

And here I faced it again. An unknown origin strike or touch or force placed upon my body, potential damages as yet undeterminable, except in the contemplation of possibilities. After a while, the paralysis of potential stacked up like unopened delivery packages, or like packed boxes moved from an old residence to a new one and left unopened because I didn't need to open boxes that housed only objects of memories not suitable in current reality. I'd forgotten what rested quietly in those boxes.

She drew memories from me, like the controllers of the overseers, in the places where I'd been consigned to the grave. Memories of loves lost and loves never gained usefully, rejected; filled of resignations from brief successes; relieved of hindsight perspectives. What could have happened. What should have happened. What didn't happen. Where the soul aches resided.

Good times, too, lived in memories there, but still, times gone by, unsaved in moments now real. In her eyes such thoughts invaded the kitchen. Slapped into the back of my head hard. My appetite for edibles dissipated, not completely, but enough for the belly bang to retreat into a pang of slight itch unnecessary to scratch, just backed up in the line of many thoughts wanting a scratch. I captured enough of my energy to move towards a side counter near the sink, backed up a step or two as allowance for some wall closeness; for at least a mental enhancement of some serenity to infiltrate into my anatomical system.

The hazy veil between us on first contact dissipated. She apparently took my retreat action to mean the refrigerator became her domain to rule. She stared at it. Sized it up. Didn't notice me at all.

I attempted a conversation moment. "Do you know me?"

"Experi? " she asked in a slight voice tone. "Is that you?"

I didn't know how to respond. I recalled no memory of her, and none of my name. Thought I might remember it. Still, her scent recalled a pleasure I'd long forgotten. Don't know how to describe it except as passion. Sudden stimulation frightening it was, her smell, more so her touch, and now her voice stimulated me in specific ways. The more I focused on these moments, the familiarity of such feelings felt somewhat comfortable.

"Tal. My name is Tal," she said.

"Tal," I said. "How do you remember me?"

"You were housed in the cold rooms. I in the warm areas."

"Where?" I asked, a bit confused.

"In a factory. They didn't tell us much about the location where we worked and lived."

"How did you get here?" I had to at least ask.

"I traveled with a larger group. We went to work our shifts, and the place was empty except for some of us. Not sure why, or if something happened."

"I wasn't there?" I tried to hide my instinct of suspicion.

"No, I don't think so. We looked for food boxes. Took as many as we could carry and walked out."

"Were you followed?"

"I don't think so. We did lose some of the group along the way. Many hungry creatures out there. Some of us made it this far, but . . . ."

"I understand. Making it this far was a miracle. How did you survive the recent assault outside?"

"I hid. Learned pretty well how to do that, and pack the food boxes at the factory."

"Humans don't usually make it this far," I remarked. She offered her perception as response.

"I'm not human, at least I don't think. Some in the travel group were humanoids, less were hybrids." Our silences and contemplation moments intertwined. She broke the ice again.

"What are you?" she asked politely.

"Hybrid," I answered, then asked "and you?"

"Not sure. Not human. Don't really know their lingo too well. Maybe a humanoid and hybrid combination."

"I sense such, too," I said.

She began to remove some of her physical fright instinct restrictions of anatomy, relaxed a bit, and began to form into her natural size. Moved from frail to a bit more muscular and taller of height, quite furry in the skin areas available to be seen, but furry flat indicating a middle age appearance. The body cloth worn reflected the factory work look that became familiar during his time spent held there. Her eyes remained as beautiful as starlight in the dark gray evening sky. I remembered that phrase from a book no longer in existence, but the words still passed along amongst generations of lips since the time they were first written. Imaginations beamed of these sights, and on rare days, the lights showed their faces as threads in the cloud blanket.

Those around me, mainly humans and humanoids, shed a few tears at these sighting moments. Not sure why, but my eyes never wet or shed tears. Perhaps engineered that way. We hoped the stars would always love us and continue their visits. Check in on us. The price for dreaming is negotiable.

Tal had me thinking. Times when I wasn't involved in social activity or conversation became dominated by memories of her pleasant voice tones, body movements, scent. My mind became captured by these memories which alerted my instincts in strange ways. During rote survival tasks my mind drifted in day dreams of our first meeting moments. Sometimes I wondered if my dreams caused her to exist, and I might awaken to discover her presence, aroma, scurry movement sounds disappeared.

She worked in one of the overseer factories, or so her voice related to me during our first encounter. Maybe they experimented on her genetic code; made alterations deemed necessary for total obedience. Still, something had sparked thoughts of her being, presence, influence upon my genetic code. Government spy? Ethereal protector spirit who had infiltrated the factory on behalf of the Wind or Shadow Souldiers? Reminded myself about how allowing emotions and feelings into mind and body could dim and dull seminal instincts.

The first Tal encounter reminded me that all previously stored memories hadn't been erased. Maybe not even replaced. Did my mind, during government instituted experiments, reject or fight off efforts needed as a defense, allowing him to retain at least a base level of survival, instead of supplication to the will of the experimenter? Then a revelation struck me hard. Memories of Aunt Helen hadn't been erased. They practically provided a road map for this new existence. The overseers had not or could not make it disappear. That's a power. Aunt Helen's power bequeathed to me during many years listening to her teachings, allowing them to swirl in my head until becoming imprinted of such tensile bond, they didn't flee despite government efforts.

I hoped this revelation led to significant truth right and proper. The weak mind avoided confrontation. Accepted the idea of an existence as pawns on any god's chessboard. Time would tell. Time never lied. Unless the overlords created a fictional time line and environment of land, sea, and air to further their path of absolute control. If dream and reality had merged, then the battle must be won along those lines. We needed to cut off the thumbs of this government. A battle for survival so demanded.

Menace, A Visit

The wind takes no prisoners. Neither does fate. The male partner of my house host returned, but not of himself only. Like the silence before a storm, he shared stories of his travels.

While once out on a hunt, he became sick, faded into an unconscious status is the best he could describe it. When he awoke in the same place, he wondered. The landscape had changed a bit. Grass higher. Broken trees limbs littered the ground around him. A sense of time change overcame him. Not sure how much time escaped him. His body tried to tell him amidst evidence of rips in the skin hairs and wear of foot pad soles. He confessed to some memories that tortured him. He believed his genes to have been crossbreed into other known but poorly catalogued species. His partner looked extremely disappointed.

"Crossbreeding isn't permitted in our culture," she said, and explained there are so few left of her species, the process was outlawed.

Then, each of them became aware of distant sounds in surrounding areas of their habitat, too regular and steady to have been emanated by a random predator's entry. Her partner weakened in breath measures.

"They took information from me. I don't think they gained much knowledge, but they've been tracking my movements. Seemed after every stop I made at inhabited parts, death followed me while I moved amidst the populations, and especially after moving on from them."

"Did you find someone to take your place, in the breeding cycle?" she asked. "Time is running out." His response in words became incapable. His body slumped into a somewhat smaller ball of fur and bone. From his arm and down into his hand ending at the fingers, he managed a directional point which concluded in destination at me.

I had no friends here, only passions for survival. Such an emotion could act like a friend. Would do as needed to help those met survive unless they portended harm. For species form, the first thought when looking at any living object involved digestibility. Such was the instinct curse, especially hybrids. Generally, larger bodies require adequate food sources and places to hide or secure to protect against prowls of other predators. Food meant energy. In times of lean food sources, beggars chose to eat. Rest slipped into memory recesses as an afterthought. Breeding to propagate a sufficiently sized clan for enhanced survival wasn't a luxury. It screamed out as necessity.

Eat or die. Breed or die out. A fairly simple equation calculated. The food chain was exactly that. A chain. Break it, and chaos ensued. The rules of biology or genetics were broken, fell to the ground, stomped into dust particles. Protocol shattered. An opportunity for chaos to rise and reign sovereign amidst the injurious flying shards. Another day in the Brim.

A situation no avian creature songs could resolve in measure, chord, key, or harmony. Pleasant sounds in communion frantic skipped to the chaos. When less than nothing is the choice, almost any situation, circumstance, proposition gains a traction along the path.

Beating heart percussionists danced to the sounds. Loves loomed as survival mechanisms dangerous. Needs had garnered a totalitarian prescience. Broken hearts mended. Scars memorialized repair. Government imposed tattoos. The gray dark no friend. Just a hovering silent doom.

Sometimes the air creatures exhibited evidence of experimentation mangling perpetrated by the overseers. If members of bird clans decided to flock and fly, an artillery barrage of doodoo served as the gray day's rain. Nuisance heavy. Some hybrids ate the grounded plops as snacks. Never be downwind near them during digestion. A knock off the pins aroma sought targets.

Woodpeckers adapted their beaks into iron and metal chippers. Sometimes we could tell if their food sources were low. They'd flock and hammer away at delivered food boxes. Many times, served as a wakeup call.

First time I tried to solve the food box paradigm; a pecker rammed me in the mid back area.

"Hey! That hurt, you drill bit." I tried to rub it but couldn't force my hand into the right spot.

"Damn it. I need a rubber." Then I thought better of the words uttered. Hoped the fairies and sprits weren't about. They were. Went below deck.

"I didn't mean it that way," I castigated them. Their tiny laugh sounds buzzed wild. Upside. They probably would spend the rest of the day high fiving the curse I had placed upon myself in their vicinity. I high tailed it for the house. Only a matter of time before rocks were maddingly flung by other residents and I didn't need to be the board of rock flings.

A raucous rapping at mechanical drill speed commenced at the nearby food boxes despite the incoming counter assault. The hungry residents used small stones to scare the peckers away, but the stone supply dwindled significantly, as if some as yet unknown creature ate the flung stones. No one could describe the eaters. Never saw them. Maybe the work of sprites and fairies. Mischief remained their pleasure.

The inhabitants developed pretty accurate rock throwing skills. These woods used to be drone search infected.

Drones flew around like overly large bees and wasps. I had more faith in a rock than the hand that tossed it, but accuracy improved with practice.

Eventually the bees and wasps disappeared due to drones crashing into them. The sprites and fairies took amusement in the goings on. They figured they could outdo the drones, rode them like horses. Not sure how they did it. No horses existed in this area. All killed off when food sources sometimes depleted, and deliveries sometimes stopped.

Maybe the government needed to retool the drones. Gave them sensitivity training, not to become safer, but for the purpose of making them more lethal during recons of the area. Eventually, the drones became extinct in this area of the Brim. The fairies and sprites mourned such a result, but easily found other amusements suitable.

Drones also had been used at traps, were near invisible until activated. The drones could activate laser beam parameters. The resident rock throwing exercise then served as trap activations. Allowed setting up markers to alert the unwary or careless.

When the drone defense strategy worked, knocking them out or disabling them completely, the government had to send flesh and blood minions out here to reset the traps.

We could spy on them, learn their competency level or lack thereof during the endeavor. Sometimes robotic, humanoid types were sent out with minions in the event the minions failed. The fairies and sprites knocked the ever-loving snot out of the robots, and enjoyed every moment of it.

Sometimes the fairies suffered casualties, generally oldlings or younglings in training, for reasons obvious. Oldlings had lost some dexterity. Younglings lacked experience. When one became hit by the beam, a pop sound could be heard. The nearby fairy kin grieved briefly but continued their mischief unabated. No graves existed for the spiritual type creatures. They moved on to the next world without moaning or fanfare. If anyone found a way to mend a broken heart, wished they would shout the method.

Need to figure out who and what you want to be, else others will decide that fate, according to Aunt Helen. She also counseled me.

"Never underestimate the tenacity of a tormentor. They've made it their job to scrounge around and unearth the strengths and weaknesses of a chosen target."

I didn't know what "unearth" meant, but while doing chores, her wisdom flowed loud, so I let her be at those work times. She unlocked my imagination trap. Ensnared it frequently as a means to help my mind better appreciate the circumstance.

This wisdom came back to my mind while taking advantage of an almost silent and rare moment, sitting on the front door's wooden stoop of my creature house host. I now imagined it as the long-ago time of youth when I rested my derriere in a seated position upon Aunt Helen's marble steps located just outside the boundaries of the summer kitchen. The marble served as access to the small but expertly gardened back yard.

"If it is crooked in angle, then it is straight in shape."

I took these words to mean anything of perfect appearance is suspicious.

She enjoyed entertaining the birds, particularly spritely finches, and on short breaks when her joints begged rest, particularly when scrubbing the tile floor of the narrow summer kitchen of food particles gone rock in solidity, she offered some advice to them. They seemed to like it, fluttering their already high RPM wings energy even more so.

"Try not to lose the connection between what is and what I like that one. Used a few senses imagined in my mind to soak the thought into it better.

"The lesser of two evils may be the easy way out of a fix, but it offered a higher rate of survival," I learned. Perhaps I heard this statement from her. Not sure. Some memories remained lost.

A Drey Moment

Some exercise our bodies ached for. No commotion sensed for now, outside. Tal and I excused ourselves from our house host's presence as the gloom of the mates death still intervened, hung heavy in the mind. We began a walk towards a bridge I wanted to explore but never made time.

"Hey. See that drey?" I asked Tal. She looked up where I pointed. Expressed a confused look. I explained a drey is a squirrels nest.

"Wow. Never seen one before. At least, I don't remember so," she remarked.

On the bridge we each looked down into the wide swath of the pond below. The clouds in the gray night sky parted and allowed a moon's appearance. Under that moon a pond reflection of the bridge appeared in the familiar upside down.

Her reflection stepped off the bridge towards the pond reflection.

"Wait!" I shouted.

She walked on the bridge along the upside-down path.

"You're floating," she said softly, looking at his pond reflection.

"I'm not," I protested.

"Look up," and she pointed.

I did so, and noticed the cloud cover hovered so low in height, my shadow could be found in it amidst slow and winding swirls. They remind me of the truth. The world is what I thought it was as a child. Totally furked up. The adults don't know what they're doing, and they get upset when their directions aren't followed. No one wants the blame, and refuses to accept it.

The worst are the politicians. Accept their mistakes, lies, thefts, crimes or suffer their wrath. They hire the media to libel and slander those who dare disagree with their edicts. They send soldiers to enforce the laws they pass to keep us enslaved; to keep our money flowing into their bank accounts.

The squirrels are serial survivors amidst such madness. They need no gods to rule them. Or at least, they've well-learned the rules of nature gods, adapted to such a narcissistic, deadly environment, and made it their own.

The nature god's rule all. No mercy displayed. Just like in the higher realms of sentients, nature takes no prisoners when the sentiments are no longer useful. The only defense for the sentients is to categorically eliminate such murders for the same reasons nature covets their own ruthlessness. Survival.

Sentients desire not just survival, but the potential pleasures evolved from it. More pleasures than just results of cunning survival methods. Nature's pleasures are instinctual needs. Food, shelter, procreation. Sentients need similar resources, but seek still more.

The more is control over all things. They want to be like the gods they've created. Noble is a fiction while survival is a fact. Turn the lights on so I can play by myself. The lights in the Brim remained always turned on. I was more confused than ever. Even our language remained unfit to describe any given moment of breaths.

"Such a pretty poison," she whispered.

Procreation Lessons

This portion of my attempted scholarly narrative dreaded me. I'd never had sex, or learned how to make love, in the manner the female portions of the varied higher intelligence groups of humans, humanoids, and hybrid creatures who engaged in such activity preferred. What was required and how to accomplish the task scared me. Just the thought of it allowed me to allow somewhat of a subservient attitude about the process. I knew nothing.

Tal and my house host would need to enlighten me. My fears reflected differently in their mannerisms identified by smirks, pats on the top of my somewhat squared off face-bearing head. I accepted these circumstances as a significant part of the learning ritual, having no other means to acquire perspective on the subject, other than the time I heard some of the humanoids in a distant village, while I passed through during my journey, emit loud sounds and moans during what seemed such a process.

Okay. A peek into their window helped me become alert to the purpose. Sex work. No, that's not right. Sex pleasures. Oh, I don't know. I would soon learn.

That children were likely to know better than I seemed odd, but asking them such a question seemed more than a bit scandalous. Didn't need scandal threads hanging from my being. The subject never came up in my presence. Only as a discussion listener, and that one peek moment, had I any clue of the ritual or specific, other than to propagate further the existing and most sentient creatures in the Brim.

First, perfumed niceties weren't necessary, just a good washing. The hybrids in heat, like my housemates, had become full of all chemical incantations and biological needs already fired up.

Second, my technique during penetration and ejaculation were important as means to bring the seed into the cavern. I mean, birth canal. Got slapped on the head for misspeaking when asked to repeat what they had explained, and frightfully, showed in mime and mannerisms. Titillation tactics failed me. The older victim, I mean subject of my faux affections, spoke more in a clinical sense. She knew how to bring the rain in such situations. The younger, middle-aged Tal, she seemed still a bit too much thrilled and enamored of the processes I was to pursue.

Finally, sounds and fury. They had me listen to verbal sounds and physical motions echoed in another of the nearby dwellings so to grasp an idea of how passion served a purpose. At least, they called it passion. Seemed more like extremely exerted effort. Important. Important to remember, then follow their leads. Do what their bodies signaled as needed.

So, we practiced a few times, separately as partners, lacking the final part of actual penetration. Fairly good preparation, I thought, but no clue how the penetration would feel and how I would react to it. Once we started the mission goal process, I realized why they hadn't told me, and why they secured the bed frame with thick and heavy ropes around my waist.

Once penetration started, I nearly projected my house host female into the wall behind the bed frame. I pulled her back at the last second as my entire body felt over-flooded with energy they previously called during lessons training an uncontrollable passion. When I pulled her upper body back towards me to protect her, she evoked a loud scream. The scary sound suddenly became sacred to my body, and I reacted accordingly, repeating such prayers in physical form, over and over until I mimicked drone activity. She moaned and screamed longer and louder. Upon reaching the level where I could no longer hold back, the conclusion erupted, the resulting sounds each of echoed of all objects in the vicinity. My eyes rolled back into my head, because a happy feeling virus infected them, and I suffered temporary blindness. And so, the first sexual experience of my beastly life ended. Too tired to eat aroused the instinct hackles in me. The poor bed mattress, I thought. Woe is it.

I won't even relate the experience involving Tal. Apparently what I first learned as an expression of passion towards her during the refrigerator incident tipped the scales of falling into a potential relationship of more than a procreation ritual. I suppose the feeling of having been complimented by each of them after the process dissolved somewhat from our minds until the usual comfort zones around us returned, unharmed. Tal's processing screams weren't as loud. Some of them evoked some painful-looking reactions, sounded like winces. She didn't relate any concerns to me afterwards, although a post event discussion happened between her and our house host once the proceedings concluded.

After the discussion concluded, Tal made a request.

"Bead me."

The demand confused me until she presented before my sight a small ring of many colors too large for a single claw, but large enough to fit over a paw and cling into her short wrist hairs. I placed it upon her wrist as requested, thinking it was part of the post copulation ritual. She patted it down against her skin to accomplish a tight fit.

"You've just declared a love for me. A lifelong attachment."

"What?" I asked, unsuccessfully hiding an agitation of thoughts. She wanted to rely on my services during future breeding rituals.

I hoped they would each give me a time frame for the gestation and birth finales, and whether any lifestyle adjustments would be needed in the future. The subject wasn't breached during training. There was a question I could hear them discuss regarding the success possibilities of the activities we engaged in. We together were not genealogically preferred breeding partners. Perhaps they plotted the future services required of me.

An odd afterthought. On the next morning, when I went outside to collect the contents of the food box, no woodpeckers, fairies, or spirits taunted me in the usual ways. None of them made a visit. I did receive some hand claps and cheers from some house residents, and an additional ovation spooned forth audibly from the windows of others fussing with their food boxes. Not sure why. Heard a shout of "way to go!" and similar accolades. One shouted comment in particular confused me. "Gone beast mode, aye?" I feigned ignorance, managed a curt smile, unlocked the food box, and began a rather speedy retreat back to the residence shared by myself and coital friends Once the air cleared about my face and head, I gave a sniff.

"I need a good washing."

Something Windy Cometh

If I've been endowed by the genes of a Shadow Souldier, then my vision should be able to focus and clarify who or what currently inhabits the area at the cusp of the tractor beam boundary. For the first time in rumored eons, a true darkness descended into that area. Something wasn't right.

I could see it, feel it, absorb it. The wind, at my back sailed light of texture, strengthened, then continued to achieve greater power and force. "The Wind Souldiers," I thought. They're here, in legion numbers as evidenced by the responses of tree limbs swaying to and froe on each side of me as far as could be sensed and seen.

I became a standing totem amidst the elements in front, at the sides, and behind. I could hear the buzz of it, feel the sting of it, but mainly it swarmed around as if directed forward and away from my hybrid creature body. The wind remained relentless of cause, embraced me again as a refill of energy source, then continued forward.

Voices of overlord controllers and soldiers began to shout, exhaling a panic storm. They are animals, like us. We just eat differently. The wind's forces heightened in fury as a tide undeterred. The shouts became voices, then whispers, and finally gasps. A solemn silence remained accompanied by somber and cooled musical wind caresses. Black darkness retreated, replaced by the gray.

The overlord swarms lay deadened, destroyed. Their bits lay spread as a party palette feast for buzzards, crows, and ravens. Boxed food packaged and ready for land animals, too. The sound of flesh locks busted, and tissue lids ripped open as a choir enthusiastic provided accompaniment to the opera bizarre. Hunger may only become served by relentless and programmed effort.

Reverence demanded screams slavery. Reverence earned beamed divine. We had defined them. Our continued existence required their destruction. They made the rules, and we followed them. Love entered as a temperamental rain storm, sudden, thunderous amidst flashes of light and eclipsed of darkness. They programmed us for our entire lives but inevitably we learned how to reprogram ourselves. They lied like a served breakfast topped off by regular whine pours.

In this place, creatures with big teeth consumed creatures which possessed smaller teeth. The pack animals, like squirrels, served as an exception. The packs worked in groups and took down threats of loners bent on harm or the weak of any size or intention. The crafty and devious government packs, poisoned by their leader schemes and skullduggery, tracked and trapped any prey they desired, first to serve their own needs, and second to pleasure desires. No more is this place shall such treachery be allowed to stand, breathe, propagate of any cause, concern, or purpose.

Desires can be incredible in scope. Needs greedy strong. Wants even more so. But desires strain to rule over all sentient beings and succumb only to nature's magic. We must resist such mind traps and distractions to permit our loved ones an ability to thrive strong, devoid of selfish traps. Desire is a fog that in time will lift and provide clarity. Just like print media, the sky cleared when the readers realized all they were reading was advertising paid for by the overlords and overseers. Particularly the parts of stories labeled as news and editorials. All prepaid advertisements from brand name to last printed period dot.

After these moments, and for much longer of the days, weeks, months, this land and lands nearby became foodless, which required migration to a larger population center. Neglect is born of victory. Government adapted. Starved more citizens of all breeds. Further miserable existence became. Even hunter breeds starved although not as expediently, except in the more united and organized communities, adaptability ruled. Tree seeds planted themselves helped by the wind, squirrels, and ground creatures. After a long time, a fruit and vegetable crop emerged as a salvation hope.

Humanoid populations showed a remarkable resilience in the evolution scales. Developed ways and means for survival. I kept my notes, to be published at another time in the hand to hand passing way.

Trust is always the issue in these matters. Such notes passed to the wrong hands, falling into government eyes possession always hovered as risk. Hybrid instincts helped to increase the odds of a maintained and stable secrecy.

The overlords unknowingly helped to map areas of danger and areas of safety. We marked and catalogued public speaker announcement locations; monitored villages and towns to assess their survival means and needs, and whether the government food boxes were dropped. The drops meant danger for our still small but growing in size clans. No drops meant an end to government surveillance in that area.

Humans remained useful as couriers, scouts, farmers, and served as warriors in a pinch. Particularly talented at working the land. Possessed a magic touch and clutch of the soil. Able to interpret and understand it. Fortunately, this part of the existence plains also remained inhabited by fairies and other spirits of wily ways. They helped us cover our tracks. Redirected paths false into bog areas ready to suck down trespassers such as overlord minions. We searched for the last train to never again, these tribulations, but it already left the station.

Observations

Many perceive this place as normal, usual to the existence plain, as if existence and the trappings thereof continued on in regular course. Previous learned and creative methods marched onward towards maintenance of continued sensibilities. Those methods dire and daft faded, then regenerated as viable in the conventional sense. We've been fooled by the fools and their overlords. Who is who and why remained a mystery. Always as if there existed two places and one of them hid missing.

Gratitude cooled many heart passions in the new Brim. It was a place where many emotions disappeared. Only what's needed to survive gains value. Still, simple pleasures remained in the places where government supervision had yet to infect. Imagination, creativity, reasoned calculations of existence systems frequented community conversations when freed from the tight grip of overseers.

Maybe one day all of our broken dreams will fade away. Where else for humans, humanoids, hybrid creatures of all stripes to hide than in homeless soul bodies? Where I am, am I. That place is a space to belong. Uninhabited preferably by a surreal government composed primarily of murder jockeys. To mock the overlords tested their chaos modes. Their ride failed to end, but their influence mechanisms had been harshly exposed. Their power structures and subunits somewhat disassembled by disappearing their anti-social Brim infected puzzle pieces. The populace in large part evolved as the social disease haunting the government's body politic.

Some of us wished our overlords to disappear into the afterlife, but speculated on the inevitable destination point. Some places existed where they could be welcomed. Some places they would likely suffer the wages of persecution as a mirrored effect of unkind and irrational deeds planned and perpetrated.

In fantasy, a true love resides. An available love lives in acts real, afflicted of sacrifice scars, bonded by mutual agreements kept, travels upon mis-stepped paths, slips and falls tolerable as long as hope remains. Young lovers don't know what they don't know. Older ones incorporated the lessons into mind and soul.

Those who can forgive and change still have a chance along the forgiven path. Broken love bonds still achieve success among the gene pool waters, along another path. Starting over takes courage and strength. Once bonds are made any outcome is possible. Memories weaved into whole cloth warm better. I will love them, memories made, as long as forever lasts.

There's always a price for dreaming. Pangs and pains of loss I feel now. Unfamiliar how to deal with such diseases. Tal and my house host try to help me understand. They use words that give no meaning to me. I will try to understand. Still mostly thinking of what is needed for survival. For them, for our new clan, for me.

Who am I? Still don't know in any measured certainty. I'm not who I was, either physically, mentally, or spiritually. Explore now who I am as a means to develop a future sociable hybrid creature status. If all the battles are won and victory means a firm seizure of identity, then victory will still remain elusive if the rules of existence are changed daily. The old have grown much immune to overlord trickery but the young still exist in the sights of such swindles. When reality sucks, then fantasy becomes preferred pseudo reality. Control is everything.

The Brim Condition

Entrance into a life form viable is almost immediately accompanied by endless repeated shifting, belching, gasping for air too frequently, and many times reaches a condition under similar ejection accomplishment. Many political enemas needed. Call it life's music.

We lose ourselves eventually in dreams of grandeur buttressed by somewhat satisfied needs for physical shelter, interjections of varied dubious knowledge decrees, forwarded by more experienced shiftiness. Then the end happens in a scene much similar to the birth beginning. What happens in the between serves as mysterious math, debated stupid by humanists, scientists for what they are worth, morals precarious certified, and otherwise, regular cajoles and shines from marketers amid news media creeps. The loudspeakers blare in madness.

Harm is good. Worrying is healthy. Lies expose truths. Lie for us. Die for us. One, two, three. None. The sun hides. Choose times. Post notes. Chronicle all. Ledgers neat. Shout sweet. When the government asks, "What did you say?" Answer, "What did you hear?" The death stroke to their sentience may last for a few moments, but they will recover breath. The good, the bad, and the either. The fugly vanished in the ether.

Calm moments occasionally intercede upon this morose mess of hoarse prophecy projected by similar folk chained to the railed upon path. Pass the wine, or a frothy beer, a tasty form of smoking materials, the chow of choice, some knowledge to success gems, and the carnage and will to tick into the mess of it all, to tuck the curtains torn from the moored rods, scrunch up and amid their sordid wrinkles.

Remained to learn the friendship classic required. Let it prick and stick the mind muscles, pounded by the magical inspirations of community, civility, in the times when it leeched from the whirlpool of the old Brim condition as whole, and not as poison spread by conniving otherworld thieves of soul sparks enlightened. The ghosts of my ancestors continued efforts to enlighten me further. Aunt Helen most frequently visited my mind.

My promise to Tal and my friendly house host creature, to protect and serve as warrior and propagator of next generation kin, I practiced reminders of, so I wouldn't abandon them in the rough days ahead during searches for sanctuary. Tal's wrist band, my creature friends educated aroma and calm demeanor helped soothe and focus my spirits. I noticed some sprites were following us during the last village evacuation and stayed on for at least this passing amount of time. I would speak with them, or at least in their vicinity to allow myself and them brief spirit essence sharing energetic. We shared stories, performed brief plays of life and circumstance.

Love's Grind and Beauty

Sometimes love sucks eggs. Rotten eggs. Difficult taste, to animate. Body into mind. Sometimes love is like a favorite meal. Tempting aromas pasted warm like soft winter land coatings. Sometimes love brings an affirmation to the inner warmth of freedom comforts. Miracles are genuinely unfathomable. Coincidences melded. Creative creature conceivable oddity.

Tomorrow Hallowed

Happiness or sorrow places propagate. Too much of one. Not enough of the other. Constant chaos conflict. Choose. The choice curse lives.

I wondered who the gods were betting on. Wager wise from secreted safety. Nature thinks we are nothing but food. Birthed into a place of careful stalks, death larks sing odes to life and dark, light and bleak, soldiers strong and soldiers weak.

The Beckoning

Just one more day is worth the cost of another breath, worth the battle in a Brim world death. Upon such a thought revelation, my eyes became wet. The wetness tickled, then stung, and finally a single drop pulled by gravity drew a line I could feel progress downward across my right cheek. Evolving still, I guess.

Time is a jealous master. It will punish life over the slightest indiscretion. Time is a beautiful servant. It provides knowledge, meditation, purpose, opportunity. It never gives up the chase. Leader of the universe and perhaps the most adequate representation of gods and power. An acorn clutched to the cosmos tree until fertilized for release upon the below world.

According to my great aunt Helen, as she foresaw, I may be crazy, but I'm not insane. And I'm not alone. She granted me her time. Taught me her skills and methods. The memories remain, just tweaked a bit as greater understanding grows.

Still not certain of my name but appreciative of my new friends' assistances. I found a path worthy and a purpose useful. Now to contemplate an answer for the ultimate question. What does a squirrel do at night?

The Close

Books by Mike Gutowski:

Cratch

Time for the Dead: Zombies-A Love Story

Ariadne

Misfortunes Of Mister Knack

Seventh Ratica

available on Amazon.com